NCHARTED VOID

TAVIK MOUNTAINS

DRYGGA ICE SHELF

ANGE

E SHELF

TES OF

lte

LOF

CLOUDMAKER MOUNTAIN

IKAYA THE ICE FORTRESS

SCALE IN MILES

0   50

0   25   50   75   100 125 150

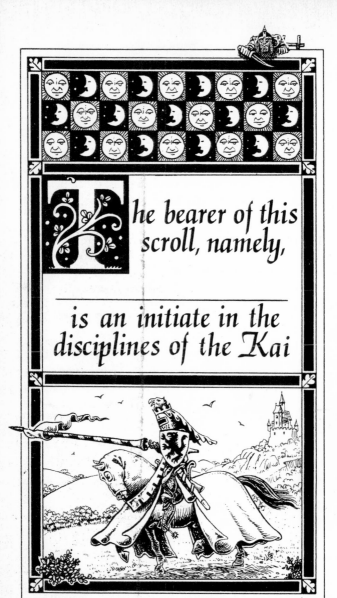

The bearer of this scroll, namely,

is an initiate in the disciplines of the Kai

Pacer

You are Lone Wolf—last of the Kai Lords. You have defeated the Darklords and saved your land from their devastation. But Vonotar the Traitor has escaped to the frozen wastes of Kalte and now rules over the Ice Barbarians. Your people demand that Vonotar be made to pay for his treachery. So great is the outcry that the King is obliged to promise that the evil traitor will be brought back to Holmgard, and made to stand trial for his crimes. For you, Lone Wolf, the King's promise is the start of a quest that will pit you against a hated foe, deep within the dangerous Caverns of Kalte.

JOE DEVER is a contributing editor to *White Dwarf*, Britain's leading fantasy games magazine. The Lone Wolf series is the culmination of seven years of research and involvement with the unique world of fantasy. He is currently at work on a huge compendium based on the world of Magnamund.

GARY CHALK was working as a children's book illustrator when he became involved in adventure gaming, an interest which eventually led to the creation of several successful games. He is the inventor/illustrator of some of Britain's biggest-selling fantasy games.

Also available in
the LONE WOLF series
from Pacer Books:

FLIGHT FROM THE DARK
FIRE ON THE WATER

Book 3

The Caverns of Kalte

Joe Dever and Gary Chalk

Pacer BOOKS FOR YOUNG ADULTS

BERKLEY BOOKS, NEW YORK

This Berkley/Pacer book contains the complete
text of the original edition.

THE CAVERNS OF KALTE

A Berkley/Pacer Book, published by arrangement
with Hutchinson Publishing Group, Ltd.

PRINTING HISTORY
Berkley/Pacer edition / July 1985

ISBN: 0-425-08407-8
RL: 8.3

Pacer is a trademark belonging to
The Putnam Publishing Group.

A BERKLEY BOOK ® TM 757,375
Berkley Books are published by The Berkley Publishing Group,
200 Madison Avenue, New York, New York 10016.
The name "BERKLEY" and the stylized "B" with design
are trademarks belonging to Berkley Publishing Corporation.
PRINTED IN THE UNITED STATES OF AMERICA

FOR CAROLINE SHELDON

ACTION CHART

KAI DISCIPLINES   NOTES

1	
2	
3	
4	
5	

BONUS KAI DISCIPLINES

6	
6th Discipline if you've completed one Lone Wolf adventure successfully	
7	
7th Discipline if you've completed two Lone Wolf adventures successfully	

BACKPACK (max. 8 articles)	MEALS
1	
2	
3	−3 EP if no Meal available
4	when instructed to eat.
5	BELT POUCH Containing Gold Crowns (50 maximum)
6	
7	
8	
Can be discarded when not in combat.	

EP = ENDURANCE POINTS   CS = COMBAT SKILL

(SEE OVER PAGE FOR SPECIAL ITEMS)

COMBAT SKILL	ENDURANCE POINTS
19	28
	Can never go above initial score 0 = dead

COMBAT RECORD

ENDURANCE POINTS   **ENDURANCE POINTS**

LONE WOLF	COMBAT RATIO	ENEMY
LONE WOLF	COMBAT RATIO	ENEMY
LONE WOLF	COMBAT RATIO	ENEMY
LONE WOLF	COMBAT RATIO	ENEMY
LONE WOLF	COMBAT RATIO	ENEMY
LONE WOLF	COM	

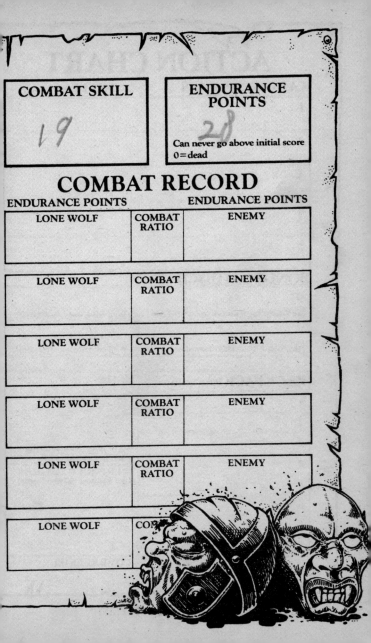

ACTION CHART

KAI DISCIPLINES   NOTES

1	
2	
3	
4	
5	

BONUS KAI DISCIPLINES

6
6th Discipline if you've completed one Lone Wolf adventure successfully
7
7th Discipline if you've completed two Lone Wolf adventures successfully

BACKPACK (max. 8 articles)	MEALS
1	
2	
3	— 3 EP if no Meal available
4	when instructed to eat.
5	BELT POUCH Containing Gold Crowns (50 maximum)
6	
7	
8	
Can be discarded when not in combat.	

EP = ENDURANCE POINTS   CS = COMBAT SKILL

(SEE OVER PAGE FOR SPECIAL ITEMS)

COMBAT SKILL	ENDURANCE POINTS
	Can never go above initial score 0 = dead

COMBAT RECORD

ENDURANCE POINTS		ENDURANCE POINTS
LONE WOLF	COMBAT RATIO	ENEMY
LONE WOLF	COMBAT RATIO	ENEMY
LONE WOLF	COMBAT RATIO	ENEMY
LONE WOLF	COMBAT RATIO	ENEMY
LONE WOLF	COMBAT RATIO	ENEMY
LONE WOLF	COMB

SPECIAL ITEMS
AND WEAPONS LIST

DESCRIPTION	KNOWN EFFECTS

WEAPONS (maximum 2 Weapons)
1
2

If holding Weapon and appropriate Weaponskill in combat +2 CS.
If combat entered carrying no Weapon −4 CS.

THE STORY SO FAR . . .

In the northern land of Sommerlund, it had been the custom for many centuries to send the children of the Warrior Lords to the monastery of Kai. There they were taught the skills and disciplines of their noble fathers.

You are Lone Wolf, and you are now the last of the Warrior Lords of Sommerlund. One year ago, the ancient enemy of your people – the Darklords of Helgedad – suddenly invaded Sommerlund and completely devastated the Kai monastery. All of the Kai warriors were in attendance for the feast of Fehmarn, and all except you were massacred.

You fought your way to Holmgard, the capital of your country, where the King sent you upon a desperate quest for help. Your mission was fraught with great danger, for Sommerlund had been betrayed by one of its own magicians – Vonotar the Traitor. His agents sought to kill you at every opportunity, but your skill and strength defeated their evil aims. You returned to Holmgard at the head of a great fleet – the allies of Durenor – and destroyed the Darklord army that besieged your capital.

Much of Sommerlund was ruined by the war. The rich farmlands were laid waste and many towns were razed to the ground. But the Sommlending are a tough people and were undaunted by the enormous task that lay ahead. They set about the rebuilding of war-torn Sommerlund with such determination that now, one year later, few of the scars of war remain visible.

For the crucial part that you played in the victory, the King has bestowed upon you the rank and title of 'Fryearl of Sommerlund', a rare honour for one so young. The ruins of the Kai monastery and much of the surrounding lands are now 'Fryelund' under your protection.

Work to rebuild the monastery was about to commence when disturbing news from the north prompted the King to summon you to the capital. Many merchants, returning from the summer trading expeditions to Kalte, told of the fall of the Brumalmarc – the leader of the Ice Barbarians. The description of the hunch-backed magician who has succeeded the fierce Brumalmarc fits only one man – Vonotar the Traitor.

After the defeat of the Darklords, Vonotar escaped to the frozen wastes of Kalte. He made his way to the ice fortress of Ikaya where, through deception, he tricked the cruel Brumalmarc into adopting him as his magician. It was a mistake that was to cost the barbarian leader his fortress and his life.

The news that Vonotar still lives spreads like wildfire throughout Sommerlund. Thousands of Sommlending surround the capital and demand that Vonotar be made to pay for his treachery. So great is the outcry that the King is obliged to promise that the evil traitor will be brought back to Holmgard, and made to stand trial for his crimes.

For you, Lone Wolf, the King's promise is the start of a quest that will pit you against a hated foe, deep within the hostile Caverns of Kalte.

THE GAME RULES

You keep a record of your adventure on the *Action Chart* that you will find in the front of this book. For further adventuring you can copy out the chart yourself or get it photocopied.

During your training as a Kai Lord you have developed fighting prowess – COMBAT SKILL and physical stamina – ENDURANCE. Before you set off on your adventure you need to measure how effective your training has been. To do this take a pencil and, with your eyes closed, point with the blunt end of it on to the *Random Number Table* on the last page of this book. If you pick *0* it counts as zero.

The first number that you pick from the *Random Number Table* in this way represents your COMBAT SKILL. Add 10 to the number you picked and write the total in the COMBAT SKILL section of your *Action Chart*. (ie, if your pencil fell on the number 4 in the *Random Number Table* you would write in a COMBAT SKILL of 14.) When you fight, your COMBAT SKILL will be pitted against that of your enemy. A high score in this section is therefore very desirable.

The second number that you pick from the *Random Number Table* represents your powers of ENDURANCE. Add 20 to this number and write the total in the ENDURANCE section of your *Action Chart*. (ie, if your pencil fell on the number 6 on the *Random Number Table* you would have 26 ENDURANCE points.)

If you are wounded in combat you will lose ENDURANCE points. If at any time your ENDURANCE points fall to zero, you are dead and the adventure is over. Lost ENDURANCE points can be regained during the course of the adventure, but your number of ENDURANCE points can never rise above the number you started with.

If you have successfully completed any of the previous adventures in the Lone Wolf series, you will already have your Combat Skill, Endurance Points and Kai Disciplines which you can now carry over with you to Book 3. You may also carry over any Weapons and Special Items that you held at the end of your last adventure, and these should be entered on your new Action Chart (you are still limited to two Weapons and eight Backpack Items).

You may choose one bonus Kai Discipline to add to your Action Chart for every Lone Wolf adventure you have successfully completed; then read the section on equipment for Book 3 carefully.

KAI DISCIPLINES

Over the centuries, the Kai monks have mastered the skills of the warrior. These skills are known as the Kai Disciplines, and they are taught to all Kai Lords. You are a Kai initiate which means that you have learnt

12

only *five* of the skills listed below. The choice of which five skills these are, is for you to make. As all of the disciplines will be of use to you at some point on your perilous quest, pick your five with care. The correct use of a discipline at the right time can save your life.

When you have chosen your five disciplines, enter them in the Kai Discipline section of your *Action Chart*.

Camouflage

This discipline enables a Kai Lord to blend in with his surroundings. In the countryside, he can hide undetected among trees and rocks and pass close to an enemy without being seen. In a town or city, it enables him to look and sound like a native of that area, and can help him to find shelter or a safe hiding place.

If you choose this skill, write 'Camouflage' on your *Action Chart*.

Hunting

This skill ensures that a Kai Lord will never starve in the wild. He will always be able to hunt for food for himself except in areas of wasteland and desert. You are aware that most of Kalte is an icy desert and that opportunities for successful hunting will not arise. But this skill is still very useful for it also enables a Kai Lord to move with great speed and dexterity.

If you choose this skill, write 'Hunting' on your *Action Chart*.

Sixth Sense

This skill may warn a Kai Lord of imminent danger. It may also reveal the true purpose of a stranger or strange object encountered in your adventure.

If you choose this skill, write 'Sixth Sense' on your *Action Chart*.

Tracking

This skill enables a Kai Lord to make the correct choice of a path in the wild, to discover the location of a person or object in a town or city and to read the secrets of footprints or tracks.

If you choose this skill, write 'Tracking' on your *Action Chart*.

Healing

This discipline can be used to restore ENDURANCE points lost in combat. If you possess this skill, you may restore 1 ENDURANCE point to your total for every numbered section of the book you pass through in which you are not involved in combat. (This is only to be used after your ENDURANCE has fallen below its original level.) Remember that your ENDURANCE cannot rise above its original level.

If you choose this skill, write 'Healing: + 1 ENDURANCE point for each section without combat' on your *Action Chart*.

Weaponskill

Upon entering the Kai monastery, each initiate was taught to master one type of weapon. If Weaponskill is to be one of your Kai Disciplines, pick a number in the usual way from the *Random Number Table* on the last page of the book, and then find the corresponding weapon from the list below. This is the weapon in which you have skill. When you enter combat carrying this weapon, you add 2 points to your COMBAT SKILL.

0 = DAGGER

1 = SPEAR

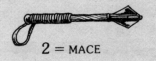

2 = MACE

3 = SHORT SWORD

4 = WARHAMMER

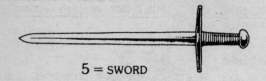

5 = SWORD

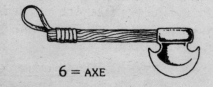

6 = AXE

7 = SWORD

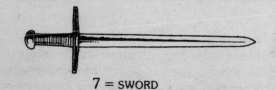

8 = QUARTERSTAFF

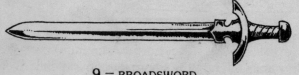

9 = BROADSWORD

The fact that you are skilled with a weapon does not mean that you set out on this adventure carrying it, but you will have opportunities to acquire weapons in the course of your adventure. You cannot carry more than 2 weapons.

If you choose this skill, write 'Weaponskill in ———— + 2 COMBAT SKILL points if this weapon carried' on your *Action Chart.*

Mindshield

Vonotar and many of the evil creatures under his command have the ability to attack you using their Mindforce. The Kai Discipline of Mindshield prevents you from losing any ENDURANCE points when subjected to this form of attack.

If you choose this skill, write 'Mindshield: no points lost when attacked by Mindblast' on your *Action Chart.*

Mindblast

This enables a Kai Lord to attack an enemy using the force of his mind. It can be used at the same time as normal combat weapons and adds two extra points to your COMBAT SKILL. Not all the creatures encountered on this adventure will be harmed by Mindblast. You will be told if a creature is immune.

If you choose this skill, write 'Mindblast: + 2 COMBAT SKILL points' on your *Action Chart.*

Animal Kinship

This skill enables a Kai Lord to communicate with some animals and to be able to guess the intentions of others.

17

If you choose this skill, write 'Animal Kinship' on your *Action Chart*.

Mind Over Matter

Mastery of this discipline enables a Kai Lord to move small objects with his powers of concentration.

If you choose this skill, write 'Mind Over Matter' on your *Action Chart*.

If you successfully complete the mission as set in Book 3 of Lone Wolf, you may add a further Kai Discipline of your choice to your *Action Chart* in Book 4. This additional skill, together with your six or seven other skills and any Special Items that you have picked up in Books 1, 2 and 3, may then be used in the next adventure of the Lone Wolf series which is called *The Chasm of Doom*.

EQUIPMENT

Before leaving the northern port of Anskavern, you are escorted to the City Hall and equipped with special winter boots, a tunic, a fur-lined cloak and mittens. You are given a map of Kalte (see the front of this book) and a pouch of gold. To find out how much gold is in the pouch, pick a number from the *Random Number Table*. Now add 10 to the number you have picked. The total equals the number of Gold Crowns inside the pouch, and you may now enter this number in the 'Gold Crowns' section of your *Action Chart*. (If you have successfully completed previous Lone Wolf adventures, you may add this sum to the total of any Crowns you may already possess. Remember you can only carry fifty Crowns.)

Before you set sail, you are given the choice of the following items (in addition to those you already possess, but remember you may only carry two weapons). You may take any two of the following:

SWORD (Weapons)
SHORT SWORD (Weapons)
PADDED LEATHER WAISTCOAT (Special Items). This adds 2 ENDURANCE points to your total

SPEAR (Weapons)
MACE (Weapons)
WARHAMMER (Weapons)
AXE (Weapons)
POTION OF LAUMSPUR (Backpack Items). This restores 4 ENDURANCE points to your total when swallowed after combat. There is only enough for one dose.

QUARTERSTAFF (Weapons)
SPECIAL RATIONS (Meals). This counts as one meal. (See 'Food' on page 22 before deciding.)

BROADSWORD (Weapons)

List the two items that you choose on your *Action Chart*, under the heading given in brackets, and make a note of any effect they may have on your ENDURANCE points or COMBAT SKILL.

How to carry equipment

Now that you have your equipment, the following list shows you how it is carried. You don't need to make notes but you can refer back to this list in the course of your adventure.

SWORD – carried in the hand.
SHORT SWORD – carried in the hand.
PADDED LEATHER WAISTCOAT – worn on the body.
SPEAR – carried in the hand.
MACE – carried in the hand.
WARHAMMER – carried in the hand.
AXE – carried in the hand.
POTION OF LAUMSPUR – carried in the Backpack.
QUARTERSTAFF – carried in the hand.
SPECIAL RATIONS – carried in the Backpack.
BROADSWORD – carried in the hand.

How much can you carry?

Weapons
The maximum number of weapons that you may carry is *two*.

Backpack Items
These must be stored in your Backpack. Because space is limited, you may only keep a maximum of eight articles, including Meals, in your Backpack at any one time.

Special Items

Special Items are not carried in the Backpack. When you discover a Special Item, you will be told how to carry it.

Gold Crowns

These are always carried in the Belt Pouch. It will hold a maximum of fifty Crowns.

Food

Food is carried in your Backpack. Each Meal counts as one item.

Any item that may be of use and can be picked up on your adventure and entered on your *Action Chart* is given capital letters in the text. Unless you are told it is a Special Item, carry it in your Backpack.

How to use your equipment

Weapons

Weapons aid you in combat. If you have the Kai Discipline of Weaponskill and the correct weapon, it adds 2 points to your COMBAT SKILL. If you enter a combat with no weapons, deduct 4 points from your COMBAT SKILL and fight with your bare hands. If you find a weapon during the adventure, you may pick it up and use it. (Remember you can only carry two weapons at once.)

Backpack Items

During your travels you will discover various useful items which you may wish to keep. (Remember you can only carry a maximum of eight items in your Backpack at any time.) You may exchange or discard them at any point when you are not involved in combat.

Special Items
Each Special Item has a particular purpose or effect. You may be told this when the item is discovered, or it may be revealed to you as the adventure progresses.

Gold Crowns
The currency of Sommerlund is the Crown, which is a small gold coin. Gold is especially valuable in Kalte, and you may find that your Gold Crowns will come in useful, especially if used as a bribe.

Food
Stored on your ice-sledge along with your tent and other equipment, is enough food for you to complete your mission. If this food, or any you may have in your Backpack, is unavailable to you when you are instructed to eat a Meal, you will lose 3 ENDURANCE points. As Kalte is an icy desert you will be unable to use the Kai Discipline of Hunting to obtain a Meal (see 'Hunting' in Kai Discipline section).

Potion of Laumspur
This is a healing potion that can restore 4 ENDURANCE points to your total when swallowed after combat. There is only enough for one dose. If you discover any other potions during the adventure, you will be informed of their effect. All potions are Backpack Items.

RULES FOR COMBAT

There will be occasions during your adventure when you have to fight an enemy. The enemy's COMBAT SKILL and ENDURANCE points are given in the text. Lone Wolf's aim in the combat is to kill the enemy by reducing his ENDURANCE points to zero while losing as few ENDURANCE points as possible himself.

At the start of a combat, enter Lone Wolf's and the enemy's ENDURANCE points in the appropriate boxes on the Combat Record section of your *Action Chart*.

The sequence for combat is as follows:

1. Add any extra points gained through your Kai Disciplines to your current COMBAT SKILL total.

2. Subtract the COMBAT SKILL of your enemy from this total. The result is your *Combat Ratio*. Enter it on the *Action Chart*.

Example

Lone Wolf (COMBAT SKILL 15) is ambushed by a Winged Devil (COMBAT SKILL 20). He is not given the opportunity to evade combat, but must stand and fight as the creature swoops down on him. Lone Wolf has the Kai Discipline of Mindblast to which the Winged Devil is not immune, so he adds 2 points to his COMBAT SKILL giving a total COMBAT SKILL of 17.

He subtracts the Winged Devil's COMBAT SKILL from his own, giving a *Combat Ratio* of −3. (17 − 20 = −3). −3 is noted on the *Action Chart* as the *Combat Ratio*.

3. When you have your *Combat Ratio*, pick a number from the *Random Number Table*.

4. Turn to the *Combat Results Table* on the inside back cover of the book. Along the top of the chart are shown the *Combat Ratio* numbers. Find the number that is the same as your *Combat Ratio* and cross-reference it with the random number that you have picked (the random numbers appear on the side of the chart). You now have the number of ENDURANCE points lost by both Lone Wolf and his enemy in this round of combat. (*E* represents points lost by the enemy; *LW* represents points lost by Lone Wolf.)

Example

The *Combat Ratio* between Lone Wolf and Winged Devil has been established as −3. If the number taken from the *Random Number Table* is a 6, then the result of the first round of combat is:

Lone Wolf loses 3 ENDURANCE points
Winged Devil loses 6 ENDURANCE points

5. On the *Action Chart*, mark the changes in ENDURANCE points to the participants in the combat.

6. Unless otherwise instructed, or unless you have an option to evade, the next round of combat now starts.

7. Repeat the sequence from Stage 3.

This process of combat continues until the ENDURANCE points of either the enemy or Lone Wolf are reduced to zero, at which point the one with the zero score is declared dead. If Lone Wolf is dead, the adventure is over. If the enemy is dead, Lone Wolf proceeds but with his ENDURANCE points reduced.

A summary of Combat Rules appears on the page after the *Random Number Table.*

Evasion of combat

During your adventure you may be given the chance to evade combat. If you have already engaged in a round of combat and decide to evade, calculate the combat for that round in the usual manner. All points lost by the enemy as a result of that round are ignored, and you make your escape. Only Lone Wolf may lose ENDURANCE points during that round, but then that is the risk of running away! You may only evade if the text of the particular section allows you to do so.

LEVELS OF KAI TRAINING

The following table is a guide to the rank and titles that are bestowed upon Kai Lords at each stage of their training. As you successfully complete each adventure in the LONE WOLF series, you will gain an additional Kai Discipline and gradually progress towards mastery of the ten basic Kai Disciplines.

No. of Kai Disciplines mastered by Kai Lord	Kai Rank or Title
1	Novice
2	Intuite
3	Doan
4	Acolyte
5	Initiate – *You begin the Lone Wolf adventures with this level of Kai training*
6	Aspirant
7	Guardian
8	Warmarn *or* Journeyman
9	Savant
10	Master

Beyond the ten basic skills of the Kai Master await the secrets of the higher Kai Disciplines or 'Magnakai'. By acquiring the wisdom of the Magnakai, a Kai Lord can progress towards the ultimate achievement and become a Kai Grand Master.

KAI WISDOM

Your mission will be fraught with great danger, for Kalte is a bleak and hostile land and your foe is a master of cunning. Use the map at the front of the book to help you plot your course to the ice fortress of Ikaya. Make notes as you progress through the story, for they will be of great help in future adventures.

Many things that you find will aid you during your adventure. Some Special Items will be of use in future LONE WOLF adventures and others may be red herrings of no real use at all, so be selective in what you decide to keep.

There are many routes to the ice-fortress of Ikaya, but only one will enable you to capture Vonotar and return to Sommerlund with the minimum of danger. A wise choice of Kai Disciplines and a great deal of courage should enable any player to complete the mission, no matter how weak his initial COMBAT SKILL or ENDURANCE points score. Successful completion of previous LONE WOLF adventures is not essential for the success of this quest.

The betrayal of your country can be avenged by bringing the traitor to justice.

Good Luck!

1

Even before you accepted the task of bringing Vonotar to justice, preparations were being made for your voyage to Kalte. The captain of the Sommlending warship *Cardonal*, having returned from a long Kaltersee patrol, was ordered to await your arrival at Anskavern. During the night, food, ice equipment and Kanu-dog teams were taken on board. The mission was highly secret – only senior members of the crew were told the true nature of the voyage that lay ahead.

The plan is to set you ashore at Halle Bluff, drop anchor and await your return. An élite team of trusted guides will lead you from the bluff to Ikaya. Once inside the ice fortress, you are to hunt down and capture Vonotar, and then return with your guides to the ship. Your mission must be accomplished within thirty days at most, for winter is closing in and no ship can withstand the grip of the Kalte pack ice. If you do not return in time, the captain will be forced to set sail without you.

For six days, the *Cardonal* sails across the stormy Kaltersee without running into a storm; but every day the temperature steadily drops until a layer of ice covers the decks. On the morning of the seventh day, the snow-capped island of Tola is sighted on the horizon. Soon after, a light wind rises from the west.

1

At first, there appears to be little danger, but within half an hour a furious blizzard is blowing, and all sight of land quickly vanishes in the scudding drift. All day the furious gale rages. Tremendous winds slice the tops of the huge grey waves and water crashes over the decks, masts and rigging of the ship, freezing almost immediately into solid ice. The sides of the ship becoming several feet thick with sea water. It is not until early evening that the weather clears, and although the wind still blows strongly, the force of the gale is spent.

You are soon to discover that the gale has blown the ship nearly thirty miles off course, along the lip of the Ljuk ice shelf. You know that to return to Halle Bluff would waste a precious day, so you decide to land on the ice shelf and start your mission from there.

As the last of the Kanu-dogs are carried ashore, your guides tell you of the two possible routes to Ikaya from here. The first route involves a hundred and thirty mile trek to Cloudmaker Mountain and then, following the difficult terrain of the Viad Glacier, a further hundred miles must be covered before you arrive at the ice fortress. The alternative route involves a longer journey of nearly one hundred and eighty miles into the Hrod Basin, followed by a trek of a hundred miles through Storm Giant Pass to Ikaya. Even if the weather and your luck hold good, either route will involve ten days of hard trekking before you reach your goal. You should consult the map of Kalte at the front of this book before making your decision.

If you wish to attempt the shorter, but more difficult Viad Glacier route, turn to **160**.

If you wish to take the longer, but easier Hrod Basin and Storm Giant Pass route, turn to **273**.

2

To your right, you notice that a stone door is cunningly concealed by an intricate wall carving. A close examination of the carving reveals a lever.

If you wish to pull this lever, turn to **290**.

If you do not wish to pull the lever, you may continue climbing the stairs by turning to **76**.

3

You watch with a mixture of fascination and revulsion as each segment of the creature shatters and then slowly dissolves into the ice. Soon, all that remains of the Crystal Frostwyrm are the undigested contents of its stomach. To your surprise, in the centre of this mess of fetid flesh and bone, you can see the shank of a Silver Key.

If you wish to take this Key, turn to **280**.

If you would rather ignore it and look for a way to open the fortress door, turn to **344**.

4

You hide the body under the staircase and quickly search it. You discover a Bone Sword and a Blue Stone Disc. If you wish to keep either or both of these items, mark them on your *Action Chart* as Special Items. You leave the body and run quickly up the stairs.

Turn to **332**.

5 – *Illustration I*

You can see two men in ragged clothes, huddled together beside a fire that seems to be burning inside a small metal bowl. Over the flames, the skinned carcass of a small animal is roasting on a spit. The men are old and toothless, and they have a strange glint of madness in their slanted eyes.

If you wish to approach them and ask for some of their food, turn to **295**.

If you wish to attack them, turn to **14**.

If you wish to ignore them and continue on your way, turn to **132**.

6

You advance into the darkness, feeling ahead with your weapon for any obstruction. For some distance, the tunnel continues northwards before turning sharply to your right. A few feet ahead, you can now see light streaming from another portal. Beyond this a staircase descends into the dark.

I. Two men in ragged clothes are huddled together beside a
small fire

If you wish to look through the portal, turn to **224**.

If you wish to continue towards the stairs, turn to **166**.

7

Suddenly, the black slab explodes into hundreds of razor-sharp splinters of stone. Your back is grazed and your ears ring, but otherwise you are unharmed. By taking refuge in the corner of the chamber, you have escaped serious injury. It now seems apparent that the monolith was designed to guard against or ensnare trespassers. A powerful glyph, a spell of protection, must have been placed upon it by an ancient mage.

As the black dust slowly settles, you notice that a panel in the north wall has opened to reveal a darkened exit from the chamber.

If you wish to try this exit, turn to **145**.

If you wish to try to open the door by which you entered, turn to **242**.

8

The smell is revolting, and you try desperately to hold your breath as you smear handfuls of the slimy grease inside your jacket. As the oil penetrates your skin, you feel a warm glow as if you were near a fire: the more grease you apply, the warmer you become. You also notice that the awful smell is gradually fading.

'When it soaks into your skin, you lose your sense of smell,' says Fenor.

'Just as well,' replies Dyce. 'I don't think I could stand living with myself otherwise!'

Baknar oil gives excellent insulation from the bitter cold of Kalte, and it may save you valuable ENDURANCE points in the near future.

Irian regains consciousness and is soon scooping out the Baknar carcass for himself. Light is now fading fast and you decide to pitch camp in this narrow pass. You prepare a meal, and then you each take it in turns to sit watch, just in case the Baknar decide to return.

Turn to **325**.

9

You desperately fight against the agonizing pain, but it is so intense that you soon lose consciousness, and within a few minutes your will has been completely drained – you have become a helpless slave, unable to resist Vonotar's psychic commands. He orders you to pick up the Ice Barbarian's sword and draw it across your throat. Powerless to resist, you kill yourself with one quick flick of your wrist.

Your mission and your life come to a tragic end.

10

The pack contains four ornate glass vials. They hold red, orange, green and black liquids.

Which one do you wish to examine?

Red?	If so, turn to **90**.
Orange?	If so, turn to **171**.
Green ?	If so, turn to **289**.
Black?	If so, turn to **225**.

(contd over)

The pack may be used as a Backpack unless you already possess one.

> You may leave this chamber at any time and continue northwards along the corridor by turning to **126**.

11

If you wish to ask who the current ruler of Ragadorn is, turn to **141**.

If you wish to ask the name of the river that divides Ragadorn into east and west, turn to **159**.

If you wish to ask the name of the tavern in Barnacle Street, turn to **234**.

12

The equipment is quickly unpacked and distributed among you. Your share is enough food for 3 Meals, Sleeping Furs, and a Rope. Remember to mark these on your *Action Chart*, and note that Sleeping Furs take up the same amount of room as two normal Items in your Backpack.

You cannot take the Kanu-dogs with you across the mountains, and you are forced to abandon them here with the sledges. A rope is secured to each person and you set off towards a narrow pass between the dark and sullen peaks. At first, the climb is quite easy; but soon the smooth ice becomes steep and difficult to cross. A wind rises that piles drifts of loose snow against the broken ice, and visibility is quickly reduced to a few yards. The drifts are deceptive and often deep. On two occasions, you sink up to your chest and have to be dug out by the others.

That night, the tent is erected on a table of ice-covered granite overhanging a deep ravine. You are exhausted and almost fall asleep over your evening Meal. (Remember to deduct this Meal from your *Action Chart*.)

'Do you understand any of the Ice Barbarian language?' asks Dyce, trying to stimulate conversation. 'Myjavik is one of the few Ice Barbarian words I know.'

When you ask him what it means, he pauses before answering you. 'Terror . . . "Myjavik" means terror.'

Suddenly there is a tremendous noise outside the tent. It sounds like the roar of a large animal.

> If you wish to draw your weapon and investigate the noise, turn to **180**.
> If you prefer to hold your breath and keep as still as possible, turn to **259**.

13

There is a lever in the wall and a spyhole in the centre of the door. Peering through the spyhole, you see a strange sight. A man in a dark robe is kneeling in the centre of a pentacle chalked on the floor of the chamber. His head is bowed and he seems to be in a trance.

> If you wish to pull the lever and open the door, turn to **128**.

(contd over)

If you wish to leave him where he is, and continue exploring the main corridor, turn to **254**.

14

The two men stare at you in horror and fumble for their weapons.

You have killed one of them before the other attempts to fight back. He is desperate and attacks you with great fury. You will have to fight him to the death.

Ice Barbarian: COMBAT SKILL 15   ENDURANCE 14

If you win the combat, turn to **309**.

15

You carefully examine the keyhole to assess your chances of being able to pick the lock.

If you have the Kai Discipline of Mind Over Matter, turn to **185**.

If you have a Dagger in your possession, or a Bone Sword, turn to **86**.

If you do not have the above skill or weapons, you should leave the chamber and investigate the stairs by turning to **323**.

16

You only just manage to slip through the gap as the stone door slams shut. Unfortunately, if you are wearing a Backpack, two separate Items have been crushed and must be discarded here. Make the necessary adjustments to your *Action Chart*, and continue along the passage.

Turn to **63**.

17

You recognize that you are suffering the first effects of snow-blindness. Unless you act now, the more painful symptoms of this malady will soon appear.

If you wish to cover your eyes with a blindfold, and keep them covered at least until you make camp later today, turn to **62**.

If you do not like the idea of being blindfolded, and prefer to risk snow-blindness, turn to **251**.

18

As your weapon sinks into the swirling wind, an agonizing blast of intense cold runs through the full length of your arm. You lose 3 ENDURANCE points and stagger back, clutching your frostbitten arm to your chest. You have lost your weapon and the cyclone is growing stronger and stronger, forcing you to retreat towards a corner of the temple.

If you wish to try to escape towards the darkened archway beyond, turn to **211**.

If you wish to continue retreating into the corner of the temple, turn to **95**.

19 – *Illustration II*

You sprint along the ice bridge and dive for Dyce's hand, but it is too late. Barely a second before you reach him his grip falters and he plummets backwards into the gaping void. A shiver runs down your spine as his scream fades into the darkness below. You are staring helplessly into the gorge when Irian begins to shout: 'There, over there – I'm sure I saw something.'

You strain your eyes, hoping to see something, anything, but the gorge is as black as midnight. You turn to see Irian pointing, not at the gorge, but towards the western horizon. 'Look over there,' he says, indicating a ridge in the distance. Two fur-clad warriors are standing on top of a large platform of ice. They are looking in your direction, alerted, no doubt, by Dyce's dying scream.

'Ice Barbarians,' says Fenor, his voice shaking with fear. 'If they reach Ikaya before us, we're as good as dead!'

You are now fifteen miles from the ice fortress and less than three hours of daylight remain.

> If you wish to press on, in the hope that you will outrun the Barbarians, turn to **327**.
> If you wish to attack them to prevent them warning others, turn to **307**.

20

The body of the Helghast bubbles and dissolves at your feet, a vile green gas seeping out from beneath its robes. As you stare in revulsion at the decomposing corpse, you suddenly realise that this foul creature must have been sent here to kill Vonotar – there can

II.   His grip falters and he plummets backwards into the gaping
void

be no other reason for its being here. The Darklords of Helgedad crave Vonotar's death in payment for his failure at the Battle of Holmgulf, and have discovered his whereabouts. The wizard must have discovered the Helghast and imprisoned it within the pentacle until he could devise a way of permanently destroying it.

You gingerly touch your wounded throat and thank the gods that you possess the Sommerswerd; its powers have once again saved your life. Turning into the main corridor, you quickly leave behind the smoking remains.

Turn to **254**.

21

The chill air whistles past, and then you suddenly crash on to a ledge of ice, over thirty feet below. You are winded and badly shaken, but still conscious. The cries of your guides soon change to shouts of joy and amazement when they see you stagger to your feet. You look upwards to see Fenor leap safely across the crevasse. Seconds later, a rope is thrown down and you are pulled to safety.

You have lost your Kanu-dogs, your sledge with its provisions, and 2 ENDURANCE points. After an anxious discussion, your guides agree to continue the mission, although they know that the hardships will now be doubly severe. Then in the distance, Irian spots a narrow passage at the edge of the ice shelf at a point where it meets the Hrod Basin. You continue your journey, and by nightfall you have reached the shelter of this pass and decide to set up camp.

Checking the remaining food stores, you realize that rations will have to be cut by half if all of you are to reach Ikaya. You lose another 1 ENDURANCE point due to the scant evening Meal.

Turn to **325**.

22

A powerful spell is shielding this lock from your mind. You concentrate until sweat stands out on your forehead, but still you are unable to break through.

Rather than attempt to open the chest by force, you reluctantly decide to leave it, and explore the staircase instead.

Turn to **323**.

23

You are lucky. Baknar are known to sleep for anything up to three days, especially after they have eaten a huge meal. This Baknar will sleep for another twenty-four hours at least. You slip past the creature, and leave the chamber.

Turn to **235**.

24

You take careful aim and hurl the Diamond along the corridor. It bounces just in front of the Ice Barbarian and then comes to rest behind the staircase. His attention is caught by the noise and the gleam of the Diamond, and he leaves his post to investigate. You seize your opportunity to run up the stairs undetected.

Turn to **332**.

25

You notice that one of the creatures has a Triangle of Blue Stone hanging on a chain around its neck. You may take this if you wish, and put it round your neck. Mark it on your *Action Chart* as a Special Item.

Wiping your weapon, you quickly push on, in case other Kalkoth should appear.

Turn to **284**.

26

Apart from the Bone Swords, you also find a Dagger and a Mace: both carved from solid bone. The Ice Barbarians also have curious Bracelets attached to their left wrists. They are plain, without mark or inscription, and appear to be made of solid gold.

If you wish to take one of these Bracelets, put it on your wrist and mark it on your *Action Chart* as a Special Item, and turn to **187**.

If you do not wish to take a Bracelet, you may continue your exploration, and turn to **63**.

If you have the Kai Discipline of Sixth Sense, turn to **231**.

27

You stumble along the bleak rock face for nearly an hour, finding nowhere to shelter from the bitter wind. Unless you have rubbed Baknar oil into your skin, you lose 2 ENDURANCE points due to the extreme cold.

If you wish to push on and continue your search for shelter, turn to **314**.

If you wish to dig a hole in the snow with your hands, and try to shelter here for the night, turn to **205**.

28

Wiping your blood-spattered face, you stagger out of the cell into the wide corridor beyond. In the distance you can see a junction.

If you wish to search the Ice Barbarian's body, you must drag it into the light of the corridor, and turn to **210**.

If you wish to press on with your mission as quickly as possible, close the cell door and continue along the corridor towards the junction. Turn to **215**.

29

The crevasse is opening wider and wider. You see Fenor jump clear and land safely at the edge of the chasm. You too are about to jump when you discover to your horror that your left foot is caught in the sledge ropes.

If you possess the Sommerswerd, turn to **43**.

If you have the Kai Discipline of Mind Over Matter, turn to **121**.

If you have neither of the above, pick a number from the *Random Number Table*.

If the number you have picked is 1–4, turn to **226**.

If the number you have picked is 5–9, turn to **266**.

If the number you have picked is 0, turn to **312**.

30

The passage continues for a few yards before turning sharply to the east. Directly ahead, you can see light seeping from a crack in the wall. Looking closer, you see a secret door and a small stone lever. You pull the lever and the door slides open to reveal a wide, well-lit corridor. To your left, less than ten yards away, is a junction. To your right, you can see a closed stone door.

If you wish to examine the door, turn to **203**.

If you wish to head left towards the junction, turn to **276**.

31 – *Illustration III*

The statue rises slowly from the altar and advances towards you. As it comes closer, you feel an intense chill radiating from its smooth, stony skin. However, its movements are stiff and uncertain – you could easily dodge its outstretched arms.

If you wish to attack this strange statue, turn to **150**.

(contd over)

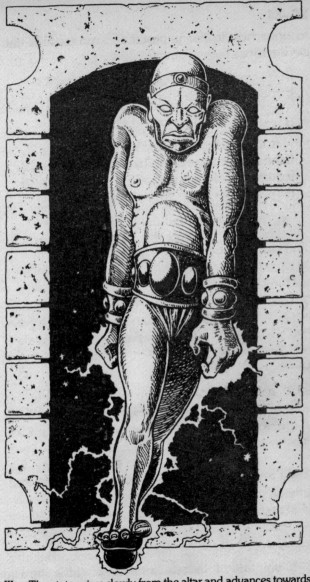

III. The statue rises slowly from the altar and advances towards
you

If you wish to dodge past it and run towards the archway beyond, turn to **306**.

32

As the creatures leap at you from beneath the waterfall, you must fight them one at a time.

Kalkoth 1: COMBAT SKILL 11   ENDURANCE 35
Kalkoth 2: COMBAT SKILL 10   ENDURANCE 32
Kalkoth 3: COMBAT SKILL 8   ENDURANCE 30

If you lose any ENDURANCE points at all during this combat, turn immediately to **66**.

If you win the combat without losing any ENDURANCE points, turn to **25**.

33

Throwing the boy on to the sledge, you grab the whip and lash the Kanu-dogs, driving them for everything they are worth. The Ice Barbarian scouts immediately give chase, shouting to the boy in their strange Kalte language.

You have covered less than a hundred yards when the boy leaps from the sledge into a deep snowdrift. At the same time, a volley of bone-tipped arrows whistle past your head, and one grazes your shoulder. You lose 1 ENDURANCE point. Although the boy is free, two scouts continue to pursue you; but your dog team is fast, and you have soon outdistanced them and their arrows.

By nightfall, you reach the very edge of the Viad Mountains. These awesome granite mountains rise vertically out of the ice and snow; they will be impossible to cross on this cold and moonless night. A wind rising in the west heralds a night blizzard. You must find shelter or you will die of exposure.

If you wish to search northwards, turn to **27**.
If you wish to search southwards, turn to **314**.
If you have the Kai Discipline either of Tracking or of Sixth Sense, turn to **348**.

34

You suddenly realize that you possess an Effigy of this hideous creature. Taking the Effigy from your pocket, you hold it before you. It begins to glow with a strange iridescence that holds the creature mesmerized. Vonotar has lost control of the creature and it is yours to command. The wizard, realizing he has lost, retreats from the moat. Loi-Kymar arrives at your side. He is breathless and is trying to say something to you.

'Use it Lone Wolf . . . send it . . . against Vonotar!'

You will the monster to capture and hold Vonotar and it instantly obeys your command. The traitor shrieks with terror and faints as the slimy tentacles close around him. You notice Loi-Kymar hurl a handful of powdered herbs into the moat. Within seconds, a mass of vines and creepers coil upwards, forming a bridge across the moat to the Brumalmarc Throne. Once safely across, you will the cretaure to release Vonotar and return to the moat. Obediently it slithers into the darkness and the crystal blocks slowly rise.

'Tie him, Lone Wolf,' shouts Loi-Kymar, as he searches for his Guildstaff. 'And be sure to strip him of his rings and amulets – he is a master of trickery. We would not want him to miss his special home-coming to Sommerlund.

You follow Loi-Kymar's instructions and make sure that Vonotar is securely tied.

'Ah! Here she is!' the old magician eventually cries triumphantly, discovering his Guildstaff amongst the tangle of vines at the base of the throne. He is anxious to leave so you thank him for his help and pass him your map of Kalte, pointing out the position of the ship *Cardonal*.

'I'll not be needing that,' he replies. 'Maps are invariably wrong; I prefer to rely on my own sense of direction.'

Loi-Kymar raises his Guildstaff and a dazzling beam of light flows from its tip. He makes three wide sweeps of the air and the Hall of the Brumalmarc is transformed into an umbrella of colour.

Turn to **350**.

35

You get an uneasy feeling that someone or something is watching you. You leave the tent and peer into the night for some sign of life, but the snow and the darkness hide everything. Reluctantly, you return to the tent and go to sleep with one hand by your weapon in case of a surprise attack.

Turn to **291**.

36

You climb over fifty steps before reaching the archway. As you catch your breath, you notice that a billowing and swirling veil of mist completely covers the arch, hiding whatever lies beyond. You suddenly realize that the temperature is much colder around this archway.

If you have the Kai Discipline of Sixth Sense *and* if you have reached the Kai rank of Guardian and therefore possess 7 Kai Disciplines, turn to **341**.

If you have the Kai Discipline of Sixth Sense, but have not yet reached the Kai rank of Guardian, turn to **124**.

If you do not possess the Kai Discipline of Sixth Sense, prepare yourself for attack and pass through the archway by turning to **264**.

37

In the darkness you have stepped into a narrow but very deep fissure in the ice floor. You fall over fifty feet and break both legs as you crash into a jagged outcrop of rock. You are unable to move and there is no one to rescue you.

Your life and your quest come to a tragic end here.

38

After ten minutes of searching the room, you discover an old fur Backpack and a long coil of Rope. You may take the Backpack only if you do not already wear one. The Rope counts as two Backpack Items, as it takes up extra space.

Finally satisfied that there is nothing else of value in this junk-filled room, you leave and continue your exploration along the east passage.

Turn to **237**.

39

So far, so good. The guards do not seem to be paying you any attention. You pretend to adjust the laces of your boot and hide the bowl behind a pilaster. You return to the kitchen and wait for the fumes to take effect. In less than a minute, the Ice Barbarian guards have collapsed to the floor, and you can approach the hall safely. To your delight, you discover that one of the magnificent jewelled doors is unlocked.

Preparing yourself for attack, you gently push the door ajar and enter Vonotar's chamber.

Turn to **173**.

40

You have fallen over thirty feet but have landed safely in a deep snow drift. Clawing the cold snow from your eyes, you are astounded by the sight that greets you. A vast cavern spreads out as far as your eyes can see: huge stalactites of crystal hang from the icy ceiling and the constant dripping of melted snow fills the air with a strangely musical sound.

You are looking upon an uncharted world that few Sommlending have ever seen, for you are staring upon the caverns of Kalte. This massive underground labyrinth was built by the Ancients many ages before the Sommlending, or even the Darklords, set foot in Magnamund. Its wide avenues, temples and halls once echoed to the sounds of a race of creatures for whom the ice was a natural home. M'lare bowls still hang from the roof, shedding an eerie, eternal light.

You follow a wide melt-water channel for over two miles until it disappears beneath a wall of shimmering ice. An ice bridge leads to a tunnel that soon splits in two.

If you wish to take the left tunnel, turn to **125**.
If you wish to take the right tunnel, turn to **184**.
If you have the Kai Discipline of Tracking, turn to **255**.

41

Removing the Blue Stone Triangle from around your neck, you press it into the granite wall. It is a perfect fit. You immediately feel a tremor running through the ledge on which you are standing, followed by the grinding noise of stone upon stone. The door opens, but after it has opened less than three feet, it begins to close.

Without a moment's hesitation, you dive into the fortress and the door crashes shut behind you.

Turn to **221**.

42

You unsheathe your magnificent sword and assail the door. A bright shower of sparks illuminates the room as each blow of the Sommerswerd bites into the ancient stone. The blade glows a fiery gold as you strike the door time and time again. The Sommerswerd will eventually destroy the door, but it may take many hours to cut a hole large enough for you to escape.

If you wish to continue beating the door with the Sommerswerd, turn to **294**.

If you wish to give up, you can leave by the previously concealed northern passage, and turn to **145**.

43

You unsheathe the golden sword and sever the ropes with one blow. Your foot is free, and you leap from the sledge barely seconds before it disappears into the crevasse. Quickly, Fenor runs to your side and pulls you away from the crumbling edge. You have lost your Kanu-dogs, your sledge and provisions, but not your life. You both jump the widening gap and join the others.

Despite the loss of equipment, your guides agree to continue the mission even though they know that the hardships will now be far greater. In the distance, you can see a narrow passage at the edge of the ice shelf where it joins the Hrod Basin. By nightfall, you have reached the shelter of this narrow pass and you decide to set up camp.

You make a check of the remaining food stores and realize that rations will have to be cut by half if you are all to reach Ikaya. You lose 1 ENDURANCE point due to the small evening Meal.

Turn to **325**.

'Follow me,' says Loi-Kymar. 'I've listened to the sounds of Ikaya for over a year, and the secret sliding doors and the hidden routes here are no mystery to me, I have learnt more about these corridors and passages from the confines of my cell than Vonotar has discovered with all of his cunning.'

You follow the old magician through a network of secret passages and tunnels, up long flights of stairs and into chambers dark and cold. At the top of one very steep staircase, you come to a stone door. A strange, sickly smell is seeping from a small spyhole. 'The kitchens,' whispers Loi-Kymar, showing his distaste for Ikaya cuisine by sticking out his tongue and grimacing.

You can see that this secret door opens next to a fireplace in which burns a roaring fire. Hanging over the fire is a large stone cauldron of gruel. Two Ice Barbarians sit at a table nearby with empty bowls in front of them.

If you possess a Potion of Black Graveweed, turn to **79**.

If you possess a Potion of Green Gallowbrush, turn to **157**.

If you do not possess either of these potions, you can open the secret door and launch a surprise attack upon the unarmed Ice Barbarians, by turning to **270**.

45

The faces of grotesque and distorted creatures adorn the surfaces of the chest. Their obscene expressions and unnatural proportions make you shudder with revulsion. Set into the centre of the lid is a large stone block carved with a hideous face, the mouth of which is shaped around a keyhole.

If you possess a Silver Key, turn to **303**.
If you do not possess this Special Item, turn to **15**.

46

You remove the Firesphere from your jacket, quickly split open the two halves and place them upon the narrow ledge behind. The Javek hisses loudly, both its heads weaving and darting at you in rage. It is desperate to attack, but it will not approach the Firesphere. Instead, it attempts to slither round the flames, but the ledge is very narrow – no more than a foot wide. It cannot pass without singeing itself. Eventually, angry but powerless, the strange reptile resigns itself to failure and disappears back along the ledge and into the passageway beyond.

You can now retrieve your Firesphere and continue your exploration.

Turn to **269**.

47

You try to pick the lock for nearly half an hour before conceding defeat. You have exhausted every possible angle and sequence, but still the lock refuses to open. Reluctantly, you sheathe your weapon, leave the chamber and investigate the stairs.

Turn to **323**.

48

The Ice Barbarian passes within six inches of your hiding place. He pauses before walking back along the corridor. You breathe a sigh of relief – you have not been discovered.

If you wish to escape on tiptoe along the northern corridor, turn to **215**.

If you wish to attack the Ice Barbarian from behind, turn to **260**.

49

You have climbed fifteen feet to a thin ice ledge. From here you have a clear view of the fissure. You think you have caught a glimpse of someone when suddenly the ice gives way beneath your feet, and you fall headlong in a tumble of granite and snow. You prepare yourself for the shock of impact, but you plunge straight into a crevasse, hidden beneath a layer of powdery snow. You finally come to rest in a deep drift some two hundred feet below the surface.

Blinded, dazed and half-suffocated by snow, you begin to claw your way out of this icy grave. When you eventually free yourself, you are astounded by the sight that greets you. A vast corridor disappears into the distance as far as the eye can see. Huge stalactites of crystal hang from the icy ceiling, and the constant drip of melting snow fills the corridor with a strangely musical sound. You shout for help until your throat becomes dry and sore, but your guides do not hear you. You still have your weapon(s), Gold Crowns and any Special Items, but you are without a Backpack, as it is still in your tent. Looking up, you see that the hole through which you have fallen is now just a tiny speck on the roof of the passage. You notice that the strange light of the ice corridor seems to come from large stone bowls hanging from the ceiling. These are M'lare bowls, a source of eternal light discovered by the Ancients many ages ago. You soon realize that your guides may never find out where you are, and quickly resolve to follow the passage in the hope of finding some other exit. After two hours of walking, you arrive at a junction where the passage splits in two.

If you wish to follow the passage to the left, turn to **284**.

If you wish to follow the passage to the right, turn to **199**.

If you have the Kai Discipline of Tracking, turn to **342**.

50

Have you located the Ancient Temple of Ikaya and found a Glowing Crystal?

If you possess this Special Item, turn to **139**.
If you do not have it, turn to **189**.

51

You sense that the Doomwolves are sleeping deeply. There is a chance that you can slip past them, overpower the Ice Barbarian guard, and close the cell door before they awake. However, you know that this is very risky and the odds are against you.

If you are brave enough to enter a cell full of Doomwolves, turn to **285**.
If you do not want to take the risk, you must leave and descend the stairs. Turn to **261**.

52

As you climb the slippery stone ramp, the sound of cracking ice makes you spin round. The large mound of crystals at the base of the ramp is beginning to move. The crystals are alive! You stare in disbelief as the mound is transformed into a writhing mass of crystal coils. The coils unwind, and the ice-creature slithers towards you.

If you wish to evade this creature and run towards the stone door, turn to **169**.
If you wish to fight it, turn to **265**.

53

Unfortunately, you mistime your dive with disastrous consequences. Both of your legs are crushed by the closing door and you slowly bleed to death.

Your life and your mission end here.

54

The glass is very delicate and it takes all your concentration and skill to avoid smashing the stem.

Pick a number from the *Random Number Table*. If you have the Kai Discipline of either Mind Over Matter or Mindblast, add 3 to the number that you picked.

If your total score is now *0–4*, turn to **250**.
If your total score is now *5–12*, turn to **268**.

55

You are less than a hundred feet from the top when the pain begins to fade. Eventually, you no longer feel anything with your hands: all sensation below your forearms is totally numbed by frostbite.

With one last effort, you reach a narrow ice shelf where you can kneel and rest. But you soon discover to your dismay that it is impossible to climb any further – you are faced by sheer walls of ice that offer no hand holds in their smooth surfaces. You will have to return the way you came. It is over four hours before the feeling returns to your hands. The frostbite is serious and you lose 5 ENDURANCE points. In addition to this, you also lose 2 points from your initial COMBAT SKILL. This loss is permanent and will affect you for the rest of your life.

It takes a further five hours to reach the bottom in safety. Exhausted and in great pain, you steel yourself to find another exit from this icy hell-hole.

Turn to **182**.

'Upon my soul, a Kai Lord!' he exclaims, his eyes now wide with astonishment.

'How I've prayed for freedom, for deliverance from this infernal place. And although hope never deserted me, I never expected such an illustrious rescuer.'

In the middle of his excitement, the old man is suddenly disturbed by a fit of coughing that leaves him pale and exhausted. It is a few minutes before he can speak again. 'My name is Loi-Kymar. I am an elder of the Magician's Guild of Toran,' he says, slowly removing a small crystal star pendant, the symbol of the guild, from beneath his tattered robes. The guild is known as the Brotherhood of the Crystal Star, and the magician shows his pendant as proof of his identity. You ask him how he came to be imprisoned here in Ikaya, many hundreds of miles from his native Toran.

'Vonotar, that unspeakable wretch is responsible for my plight. Days before the Darklord invasion of Sommerlund, he betrayed your Kai masters to win power – the black power of death and darkness. However, he failed to play his part in the war plans his evil masters had laid. The Darklords do not tolerate such weakness – mercy has no place in their brutal minds. In the bitterness of defeat, they sought to destroy Vonotar for his crime of failure. Vonotar knew that I possessed the only means to effect an escape from their vengeance, for my Guildstaff has the power of teleportation. He tried to steal it and flee to the safety of Ikaya by himself, but he learnt that its power is not for all men to share; only I am blessed

IV.   'My name is Loi-Kymar. I am an elder of the Magician's
       Guild of Toran'

with its secret. He was angry and would have murdered my kinspeople had I not agreed to bring him here, so I had no choice but to do so.

'Ever since, I have been a prisoner in this cell. Vonotar has tortured my body and my mind, but I have not divulged the secret of my Guildstaff, which he now keeps in the Hall of the Brumalmarc. For if I were to tell him, my life would no longer be of any value.'

You tell Loi-Kymar of your mission and of the events that have led to your meeting. He offers to show you a route through Ikaya to the Hall of the Brumalmarc where Vonotar now resides as ruler, and if you can retrieve his Guildstaff, he promises to teleport you to the coast in time to rendezvous with your ship.

For the first time since you fell into the caverns of Kalte, you feel confident that your mission can now succeed.

Turn to **192**.

Turn to **192**.

57

The next day is bitterly cold. A fierce northerly wind blows relentlessly, beating your face, and drying your lips until they crack and bleed. Your nose begins to run but the mucus instantly freezes on your lips. The sun is obscured by a thick layer of falling snow that mutes the light. Snow mounds and small potholes in the ice become invisible, and the journey is often brought to a halt when a sledge overturns or jams.

Great strain is put on your eyes by the constant glare as you search for the rough ice on the ground which is so hazardous. By midday, your vision has become a blur.

(contd over)

If you have the Kai Discipline of Healing, turn to **17**.

If you do not possess this skill, turn to **251**.

58

The cone of frost rips into the vines and freezes them in an instant. They become brittle and collapse under your weight. Without hesitation, you sprint across the falling bridge and dive on to the far platform just as the vines completely disintegrate.

You have made it safely across the moat, but you are now lying at Vonotar's feet. He sneers at you and points his crystal rod at your head.

Turn to **252**.

59

The Kalkoth charges on to the lake and immediately falls through the ice. Beneath the frozen surface, a shadow speeds towards the helpless creature as it thrashes wildly in the icy water, snatching it suddenly into the depths. An unnatural stillness descends and all that remains now is a large patch of red water, spreading slowly beneath the ice.

You quickly scramble towards the jagged outline of the tunnel on the far side of this lake. As you reach the solid ice of the bank, you notice something strange lying there. It is a small triangle of blue stone on a neck chain. If you wish to keep this Blue Stone Triangle, slip the chain over your head and mark it on your *Action Chart* as a Special Item.

Enter the tunnel by turning to **235**.

60

You have taken less than a dozen steps when a brilliant crackle of blue energy arcs between the two staves. You see the white statue beginning to move as if activated by the surge of power.

> If you wish to attack the creature before it rises from the altar, turn to **150**.
> If you wish to remain perfectly still and prepare for combat, turn to **31**.
> If you wish to run for the darkened archway beyond, turn to **306**.

61

You enter a covered balcony running round the perimeter of an open courtyard. Suddenly you hear the dull tone of a stone bell as it tolls in a watchtower high above the fortress – the alarm bell. The balcony and the courtyard below are completely deserted, except for a wind sledge near to the courtyard gate.

You decide to take a chance, and descend a flight of steps to discover that the sledge is loaded with food and equipment from Ljuk. With the whole of Ikaya alerted to your presence, it is now impossible to complete your mission. There is nothing else you can do but make your escape on the wind sledge, while there is still time.

Ten days from now, you will reach your ship the *Cardonal* and regretfully report that you have failed your mission.

62

As the light gradually fades, a blizzard blows across the open ice shelf and batters relentlessly against the tent. The flapping canvas and the pain in your fingers and toes are beginning to wear on your nerves; you wish you had never set foot in this icy hell. Then, in the middle of the night, the wind rips away the edge of the canvas and the full force of the gale scatters your equipment and provisions. You are forced to spend the rest of the night on your elbows, clinging with frozen fingers to the edge of the tent. Your sleeping furs fill with a half frozen slush, and, by dawn, your clothes are stiff with ice. You lose 3 ENDURANCE points. Make the necessary adjustment to your *Action Chart*, before turning to **167**.

63

You follow this passage northwards until it turns abruptly towards the west. A few yards ahead, a flight of stone steps ascends to an archway thirty feet above. Just past the staircase, you notice another stone door, with a lever in the wall next to it. The lever is raised and the door is closed.

If you wish to climb the stairs, turn to **323**.
If you wish to investigate the door, turn to **246**.

64

You get the uneasy feeling that danger lurks along both tunnels. Although you sense that the northern tunnel is the more perilous of the two, you feel sure that it is the quickest route to Ikaya.

If you wish to enter the north tunnel, turn to **235**.
If you wish to take the west tunnel, turn to **275**.

65

The buttons have jammed. No matter how hard you try you cannot make them budge. You have no choice but to abandon the altar and leave the temple by the northern archway.

Turn to **306**.

66

The barb of a Kalkoth's tongue holds a powerful venom, with which it paralyses its victims before devouring them. The venom takes only a few seconds to act. Stung by the barb, you quickly fade into unconsciousness. It is a sleep from which there will be no awakening.

Your life and your mission end here.

67

The man jerks his head back as if suddenly woken from a trance. 'Who's there?' he whispers, his deep-set eyes peering into the gloom above. 'Is anyone there, or does madness now befriend me?' You extend your hand through the portal and chance a wave to show your whereabouts. 'The Gods be praised,' he cries, jumping excitedly to his feet. 'My name is Tygon. I am a merchant from Ragadorn. The Ice Barbarians kidnapped me and my cargo, and brought me here. I now await an audience with their new Brumalmarc, the Sommlending sorcerer called Vonotar. It seems that he will decide my fate. If you free me, I'll help you as best I can.'

If you have a Rope, you can lower it through the portal and help the man to climb out of his cell by turning to **328**.

If you do not possess a Rope, or if you do not want to help him, you can continue along the corridor towards the stairs by turning to **166**.

68

As the Ice Barbarian moves closer, he suddenly lets out a blood-curdling scream and lunges at your head.

Ice Barbarian: COMBAT SKILL 18   ENDURANCE 28

If you win the combat, turn to **186**.

69

You have covered less than twenty yards when you see a patrol of six Ice Barbarians marching towards you along the corridor. Then, to your left, you notice a small flight of stairs leading down into a darkened chamber.

If you wish to run down these stairs and hide from the patrol, turn to **108**.

If you wish to run back to the landing and take the north corridor, turn to **198**.

If you have the Kai Discipline of Camouflage, turn to **222**.

70

'Quick, we must pack up and leave immediately,' shouts Fenor, the howling wind carrying his words away into the night. 'Kalkoth never hunt alone. There's sure to be others nearby – they can smell blood miles away.'

The tent is dismantled and you quickly leave, Dyce leading the way and you guarding the rear. You have covered less than fifty yards when disaster strikes. Blinded both by the darkness and the wind, Dyce fails to see that the path comes to an abrupt end at the edge of a sheer precipice. You freeze with horror as you hear the screams of your guides fading into the darkness. With death threatening from all sides, you cling in desperation to the frozen rockface.

If you have coated yourself with Baknar oil, turn to **209**.

If you have not applied this oil to your skin, turn to **339**.

71

You can sense that the Ice Barbarian child has a bone dagger hidden in his boot. He is trying to reach it so that he can attack you.

Forewarned by your Kai sense, turn to **320**.

72

You carefully examine the altar and the two black staves protruding from its surface. The cyclone continues to howl but while you carry the firesphere, it will not advance towards the altar.

You notice that where the statue once lay, two stone buttons have risen from the surface.

Turn to **227**.

73

The guides look at you as if you are mad, and refuse to ride with you. At first, the Kanu-dogs are reluctant to approach the gorge, but with some encouragement from your whip they soon change their minds. There is less than six inches of ice on either side of your sledge runners, and all your concentration is needed to keep to the centre of this frozen bridge. You are less than fifteen feet from the other side when there is a tremendous crack and the sledge shudders violently.

Pick a number from the *Random Number Table*.

If the number you have picked is *0–7*, turn to **119**.
If the number you have picked is *8–9*, turn to **136**.

74

The stone walls of the corridor are covered with strange carvings, which cast deep shadows. Using your skill, you hide yourself in their gloom. The Ice Barbarian walks slowly towards you, his movements tense and unsteady. Your skin crawls as you notice for the first time his white pupil-less eyes. Holding your breath, you pray that he has not seen you.

Pick a number from the *Random Number Table*.

If the number you have picked is *0–4*, turn to **48**.
If the number you have picked is *5–9*, turn to **287**.

75

The tracks have been made by dangerous and carnivorous creatures called Baknar. If you run into them in the confines of a dark and narrow tunnel, your chances of survival will be very slim indeed. Although your Kai Discipline has enabled you to identify the tracks, you are unable to sense which tunnel the Baknar occupy.

If you wish to take the left tunnel, turn to **235**.
If you wish to take the right tunnel, turn to **114**.

76

You continue upwards until you reach a narrow stone door. Like the other doors you have seen so far, it is controlled by a wall lever. This door also has a small spyhole cut into its centre. Carefully placing your eye to the aperture, you peer into the small room beyond. There, lying on the floor of the cell, are three sleeping Doomwolves. In the north wall, a cell door is open, and the outline of an Ice Barbarian's back can be seen filling the archway.

If you have the Kai Discipline of Hunting or Animal Kinship, turn to **51**.

If you do not have either of these skills, you can open the door and attack the Doomwolves by turning to **137**.

If you would rather back away from the cell door and descend the stairs, turn to **261**.

77

You recognize the pungent smell of distilled Graveweed, a very powerful poison. Even the vapour is enough to make your head spin and your vision blur. Quickly you discard the broken glass and cover your nose with the sleeve of your jacket; you lose 1 ENDURANCE point due to the effects of the poisonous vapour.

Return to **10** and choose your next course of action.

78 – *Illustration V*

Preparing yourself, you pull back the flap of the tent and quickly leave. The wind has become much stronger, and it whips the fine snow into small eddies, obscuring your vision. A shadow to your right betrays the Baknar as it lopes towards you. There is no time to evade its attack and you must fight the creature to death.

Baknar: COMBAT SKILL 19   ENDURANCE 30

If you win the combat, turn to **245**.

79

You open the door just enough to be able to pour the Vial of Graveweed into the bubbling gruel. You have

V.   A shadow to your right betrays the Baknar as it lopes towards
you

not long to wait for the Ice Barbarians to eat what will be their last supper. You are now free to explore.

The kitchen is small and surprisingly well stocked with herbs. 'These must have come from the trading post at Ljuk,' says Loi-Kymar, peering at the many jars and bottles. He takes several of the herb jars and crams them into the pockets of his robes. You are anxious to leave in case other guards should enter, but the old magician seems completely engrossed in his new discoveries. He opens two small jars, and mixes the contents together, urging you to eat with him. 'It will give you strength, Lone Wolf,' he says. As you eat the dry leaves, you feel a warm glow radiating throughout your body. Restore 6 ENDURANCE points to your current total.

Turn to **301**.

80

As the raging Kalkoth charges out of the tunnel, you wait until the last possible moment before you dive.

Pick a number from the *Random Number Table*.

If the number you have picked is *0–1*, turn to **123**.
If the number you have picked is *2–9*, turn to **59**.

81

You are about to hide the dead body under the stairs when you hear strange cries and low screams drifting down the corridor. A group of Ice Barbarians are advancing towards you. You are momentarily stunned by the sight of these warriors, for they are hideously mutated. With fear and revulsion welling up inside, you scramble the stairs to a wide landing where a corridor runs north to south.

If you wish to run northwards, turn to **198**.
If you wish to run southwards, turn to **69**.

82

The cave is cold and slopes very steeply away into the darkness. You have covered sixty yards before you notice a light in the distance. As you get nearer, you hear noises . . . animal noises.

If you have the Kai Discipline of Animal Kinship, turn to **329**.
If you wish to draw your weapon and charge, turn to **138**.
If you want to try to creep closer and spy on whatever is there, turn to **107**.

83

The Ice Barbarian mutants seem to be controlled by a hideous creature lurking in the shadows of a distant doorway. This monster resembles an abnormally

large human head with two feet protruding beneath. It has no torso or limbs, but has a long reptilian tail with which to maintain its balance.

The Ice Barbarian mutants attack simultaneously, and you must fight them as one creature. They are immune to Mindblast. At the same time their strange controller is attacking you with its Mindforce. Unless you possess the Kai Discipline of Mindshield, you lose 2 ENDURANCE points due to this attack.

Ice Barbarian Mutants:
COMBAT SKILL 18   ENDURANCE 24

If you win the combat, turn to **313**.

84

You notice that the Kalkoth has a blue triangle of stone on a chain around its neck. Suddenly you realize the significance of this strange amulet. Grabbing the blue stone, you race back to the fortress door and press it into the wall recess. It is a perfect fit.

You become aware of a faint tremor running through the ledge on which you are standing, followed by the grinding noise of stone upon stone. The door opens, but it has only opened three feet when there is a loud *crack*, and it starts to close. Without a second's hesitation, you dive into the fortress and hear the massive door crash shut behind you.

Turn to **221**.

85

For three days and nights, you fight your way northwards across the tortuous glacier. Falls, bruises, cut shins, awkward crevasses, razor-edged ice and the constant bitter wind all conspire to sap your strength. However, you count yourself very lucky to have avoided a blizzard, and after a fatiguing trek you eventually reach the shelter of Cloudmaker Mountain in time to set up camp there for the night.

This huge mountain is over thirteen thousand feet high, and shaped like a giant shark's fin. As the cold west winds blow around its peak, great plumes of cloud trail away across the Viad glacier. It is this strange phenomenon which gives the mountain its apt name.

You soon find an ideal campsite among the shattered fissures of the rock-strewn base. Quickly the tent is up and you are under canvas once again. You have left the tent to answer a call of nature when you discover, purely by chance, the faint glow of torchlight from a small crack in the rocks above.

If you wish to investigate this strange light, turn to **49**.

If you wish to ignore it and return to the tent, turn to **212**.

If you have the Kai Discipline of Sixth Sense, turn to **98**.

86

You insert your blade and try to locate the locking mechanism. The keyhole is unusually deep and it is very difficult to manipulate the tip of the blade successfully.

Pick a number from the *Random Number Table*. If you have the Kai Discipline of Weaponskill with the weapon that you are now using, you may add 3 to the number that you have chosen.

If your total is *0–7*, turn to **47**.
If your total is *8–12*, turn to **194**.

87

You race towards the corner where you saw the creature, only to find that the corridor turns abruptly westwards. A few yards ahead, a flight of stone steps ascends towards a dark archway thirty feet above. Just beyond the staircase, the corridor continues to another stone door. The lever in the wall by the door is raised, and the door is closed. There is no sign of the strange creature.

If you wish to climb the stairs, turn to **323**.
If you wish to investigate the room, turn to **246**.

88 – *Illustration VI*

As the two-headed serpent slithers along the ledge, you can clearly see the open jaw of its second head and the yellow, curved fangs, dripping with venom. Peeling off your thick jacket, you wind it around your left forearm. You can now use your padded arm to shield yourself from one deadly head as you strike at the other. This creature is immune to Mindblast.

Javek: COMBAT SKILL 15   ENDURANCE 15

If you lose any ENDURANCE points during this combat, do not subtract them from your ENDURANCE point total. Instead, pick a number from the *Random Number Table*. If the number you pick is *0–8*, the Javek has sunk its fangs harmlessly into your padded

VI.   The two-headed serpent slithers along the ledge

arm, and you may continue the combat without losing any ENDURANCE points.

However, if you pick a 9 at anytime, the fangs have punctured your arm. The venom of a Javek is the most powerful natural poison in all of Magnamund. In a few seconds your heart stops, and your paralysed body falls into the abyss. Your mission ends here.

If you win the combat, turn to **269**.

89

The Ice Barbarian shouts at you in a deep unnatural tone. You have been seen. Cursing your bad luck, you quickly unsheathe your weapon. Wheeling round, you see the Ice Barbarian pulling a lever in the far wall. Three snarling Doomwolves race out of a concealed archway and charge towards you. They attack you one at a time, and you must fight each of them to the death.

Doomwolf 1: COMBAT SKILL 15   ENDURANCE 24
Doomwolf 2: COMBAT SKILL 14   ENDURANCE 23
Doomwolf 3: COMBAT SKILL 14   ENDURANCE 20

If you win the combat, turn to **161**.

90

Wiping the grime from the stopper, you unscrew it and carefully sniff the red liquid.

If you have the Kai Discipline of Healing, turn to **233**.

If you do not have this skill, you are suspicious of the possible ill effects of this fluid and discard it. Return to **10** and choose your next course of action.

91

You hold your breath as you wipe handfuls of the slimy grease inside your jacket. But as the oil penetrates your skin, you feel a warm glow, as if you were near an open fire. The more grease that you apply, the warmer you become. You also notice that the terrible smell is gradually fading away.

'Once it's in your skin, you can't smell a thing,' says Irian, calling the others to take some Baknar oil. This oil is excellent insulation against the freezing temperatures of Kalte, and may well help you in the near future. As you return to your tent, only the Kanu-dogs seem to object to the smell. They whine and bury their noses in the snow as you walk past.

Turn to **134**.

92

You walk along the passage for several minutes until it takes a left turn. To your dismay, you see that a huge fissure has opened, destroying most of the walls and floor of this new passage. The gaping hole is dark and wide.

If you have a Rope, turn to **133**.

If you do not possess a Rope, you will have to retrace your steps and explore the other tunnel. Turn to **297**.

93

You struggle for nearly five agonizing minutes before your will completely drains away. You have become a mindless automaton. Unable to resist Vonotar's psychic commands to kill yourself, you throw yourself on the blade of the Sommerswerd.

Your life and your mission end here.

94

You have slipped and fallen into the icy water; the shock makes you scream out in pain as cramp bites into your legs. You fight with all the strength you have to reach the bank, but it is a desperate struggle.

Pick a number from the *Random Number Table*.

If the number you have picked is 0–6, you are lucky. You drag yourself from the icy water and lie exhausted on the bank. Lose 3 ENDURANCE points and turn to **176**.

If the number you have picked is 7–9, the icy water soon paralyses your arms and, within minutes, you drown. Your mission ends here.

95

The intense cold and relentless buffeting of the cyclone quickly drain all your reserves of strength. A numbness sweeps over you as the Ice Demon claims your body for itself, eager to begin a new and powerful existence. For the creatures of Ikaya, and eventually all of Kalte, it is the dawning of a new and terrible age of tyranny, but one which you will not live to see.

Your life and your mission end here.

96

Wrapping yourself in your white cloak, you take cover behind a stalagmite near to the lake's edge. Holding your breath and keeping as still as possible, you listen to the footsteps and growls of the Kalkoth, as they draw nearer and nearer.

To see if your Kai skill has saved you from detection, pick a number from the *Random Number Table*.

If at any time you have smeared Baknar oil into your skin, add 2 to the number you have picked.

If your total score is now *0–8*, turn to **59**.
If your total score is now *9–11*, turn to **214**.

97

This corridor is lined with arched stone pilasters, several feet thick, behind which you can hide. Twenty yards ahead, you see an Ice Barbarian warrior standing guard at the bottom of a flight of wide stone steps. Moving quickly to one side, you realize that if you are to get past this guard successfully, you will either have to distract his attention or silence him for good.

If you possess a Diamond, turn to **24**.
If you wish to distract him with some Gold Crowns, turn to **152**.
If you decide to attack him, turn to **208**.

98

You sense the presence of someone or something lurking inside the fissure, although you cannot tell if their intentions are good or evil.

If you wish to explore the fissure, turn to **49**.
If you wish to return to the tent, turn to **212**.

99

As you draw your mighty blade, a golden glow illuminates the darkness of the passage. The Helghast shrieks and steps back, its eyes glowing red with hatred and fear. It recognizes the power you wield, a power that can bring about its eternal destruction. In desperation, it attacks you with a powerful Mindblast. Unless you possess the Kai Discipline of Mindshield, you must lose 2 ENDURANCE points for *every* round of combat that you fight this creature. The Helghast is immune to Mindblast, but as one of the undead it is especially vulnerable to the Sommerswerd. Be sure to double all ENDURANCE points it loses due to the power of the Sommerswerd.

Helghast: COMBAT SKILL 22   ENDURANCE 30

If you win the combat, turn to **230**.

100

The hunchbacked traitor gasps with astonishment at your sudden appearance, but quickly regains his senses and makes a dash towards a door in the far wall. The Ice Barbarians draw their swords, but their reactions are slow and unsteady. You knock them aside before they can strike at you, and sprint after the disappearing magician.

The door leads to a landing with two staircases. A spiral staircase descends to your right, and a small flight of stairs ascends to an arch to your left. There is no sign of Vonotar in this chamber.

If you wish to descend the spiral staircase, turn to **148**.

If you wish to ascend the stairs to the arch, turn to **61**.

101

You are most fortunate that Baknar sleep long and deeply, sometimes for up to three days after a large meal. But you have now made sure this creature will never waken.

Leave the chamber and turn to **235**.

102

A secret compartment slides open at the base of the left altar staff. Inside, you discover a small statuette, a Stone Effigy of a strange tentacled creature.

If you wish to keep this Effigy, slip it into your pocket and mark it on your *Action Chart* as a Special Item.

If you wish to activate the buttons again, turn to **65**.

If you wish to leave the temple, turn to **306**.

103 – *Illustration VII*

The following day, a strong wind rises from the north. Hour upon hour, it blows relentlessly into your face. The Ljuk ice shelf becomes a mass of twisted slabs of ice, jutting upwards at every angle. Progress is slow and difficult. By midday, you are shivering with cold; your lips are cracked and bleeding and the icy blasts have covered you with a thin film of snow.

You steer your sledge through a narrow passage at the edge of the ice shelf where it meets the Hrod Basin. Here you are sheltered from the wind, and for the first time today you can see ahead quite clearly.

Suddenly, shrieks from above warn you that you are not the only creatures seeking shelter here. Within seconds, three large Baknar jump from the ice wall and land with a crash on the sledges. Your fellow driver, Irian, is thrown against the ice and collapses unconscious. You are prevented from going to his aid by a hungry carnivorous Baknar. There is no hope of evading it; you must fight it to the death.

Baknar: COMBAT SKILL 19   ENDURANCE 30

If you win the combat, turn to **305**.

104

You eventually arrive at a large stone door. Unlike the others, this has no lever to activate it, but you do notice that a small slot has been cut in the nearby wall.

If you possess a Blue Stone Disc, turn to **135**.

If you do not have this Item, you will have to return along the corridor and head south by turning to **330**.

VII.   Three large Baknar jump from the ice wall and land with a crash on the sledges

You have fallen over a hundred-and-fifty feet into a massive snow drift. You are shaken and winded but otherwise unharmed. It takes nearly half an hour to tunnel your way clear and when you finally stagger out of the powdery snow, you are astounded by the sight that greets you. A huge underground cavern spreads into the distance. Stalactites of crystal hang from the icy ceiling and the constant dripping of melting snow fills this ice world with an eerie, musical sound. You are looking at an uncharted world that few Sommlending have ever seen, for you have fallen into the caverns of Kalte. This chamber is a tiny part of a massive underground labyrinth built by the Ancients, many ages before the Sommlending or even the Darklords set foot in Magnamund. Its wide avenues, temple and halls once echoed with the sound of a race of creatures for whom the ice was a natural home. M'lare bowls still hang from the roof, bathing the chamber with their eternal light.

You shout towards the opening high above, but there is no reply. Irian and Fenor have given you up for dead, and they are now trying to make their way back to the *Cardonal*.

The sides of the cave are steep and sheer. To climb up to the surface from here would be impossible. In the distance, to the north, you notice a rough-hewn tunnel. There is also a similar tunnel to the west.

If you wish to explore the north tunnel, turn to **321**.

If you wish to explore the west tunnel, turn to **275**.

If you have the Kai Discipline of Sixth Sense, turn to **64**.

106

As you leap to your feet, you see three Ice Barbarians advancing towards you along the corridor. The fur-clad warriors are armed with vicious bone swords, each encrusted with sharp teeth along the blade. Even in the surprise of their attack you notice the strangeness of their eyes: they are completely white and have no pupils at all.

They attack you as if they were possessed of one mind, lunging at you simultaneously and dodging your blows in unison. You must fight them as one enemy. They are immune to Mindblast.

Ice Barbarians: COMBAT SKILL 19   ENDURANCE 36

You may evade at any time by crawling back into the chamber and escaping by the north passage. Turn to **145**.

If you win the combat, turn to **338**.

107

As you peer into the large ice cavern beyond, you are horrified to see three large, ugly creatures fighting and clawing at each other. They are fighting over the mutilated carcass lying at their feet. They are Kalkoth, savage predators of Kalte.

If you have smeared Baknar oil into your skin, turn to **202**.

If you have not coated yourself with Baknar oil, you can avoid the Kalkoth by retracing your steps back to the other tunnel. Turn to **284**.

(contd over)

If you wish to attack the squabbling creatures, turn to **138**.

108

You see the patrol march past and you wait until their footsteps start to fade before you climb the stairs. A sudden cry from inside the chamber startles you, and you spin round to see an Ice Barbarian looming out of the dark. He is attacking you with a bone-tipped spear.

Ice Barbarian: COMBAT SKILL 16   ENDURANCE 24

You can evade combat after one round by running up the stairs.

If, at this time, you wish to head south (right), turn to **330**.

If you wish to head north (left), turn to **198**.

If you win the combat, turn to **282**.

109

Your attack is swift and deadly. Neither of the Kalkoth will ever wake from their sleep. You make a quick search of the cavern floor but find nothing of value. A growl in the distance makes you anxious, and you quickly leave via the north tunnel.

Turn to **235**.

110

The stone door grinds open to reveal a small, dimly-lit chamber. A black monolith, eight feet high, stands directly in front of you. It is covered with strange symbols. You advance to get a clearer look, when the door suddenly begins to close behind you. There is no lever inside this chamber.

If you wish to take a dive through the shrinking gap, turn to **283**.

If you prefer to stay where you are, turn to **256**.

111

The door slides open to reveal a wide, well-lit corridor running north to south. The low rumbling noise you detected earlier seems much louder here than in the darkness of the passage behind. To your left you see a door and in the distance, a junction.

If you wish to investigate the junction, turn to **254**.

If you decide to close the secret door and to continue exploring the dark tunnel, turn to **336**.

112

Before you all bed down for the night in your warm sleeping furs, Fenor prepares a nutritious Meal of dried meat in Wanlo, a potent spirit.

With the strong wind beating upon the roof of the tent, you slip into a deep sleep. But your dreams are nightmares filled with ghastly images of Vonotar the Traitor.

Turn to **291**.

113

Your lightning reactions have enabled you to avoid being crushed by the closing door. You adjust your equipment and set off along the corridor.

Turn to **63**.

114

You have covered less than fifty yards when you arrive at another cavern. Lying upon a raised dais of ice in the centre of the frozen chamber is a Baknar, a fierce and carnivorous ice creature. It seems to be sound asleep and the remains of an animal lie scattered around the slab. In the far wall of the chamber lies another tunnel.

If you wish to creep stealthily past the Baknar, turn to **23**.

If you wish to attack the creature, turn to **101**.

If you have the Kai Discipline of Hunting, turn to **279**.

115

You discover that many of the bones scattered among the stalagmites are of human origin. Shattered skulls, skeletal hands and rib cages lie half buried in the ice. You are about to abandon your search when a small box made of carved bone catches your eye.

If you wish to open this box, turn to **218**.

If you prefer to leave it, you can examine the fortress door by turning to **52**.

116

You pour the healing Potion on to your sore and broken skin. Immediately, you feel the soothing effects of the fluid. The pain fades and the swelling begins to subside. The Glowing Gem is a cursed Doomstone, and the power it contains is deadly to all living creatures. Had you not possessed a Laumspur Potion, the effects of the Doomstone would certainly have killed you. You discard the deadly Gem and the now empty Vial of Laumspur.

Make the necessary adjustments to your *Action Chart* and continue along the corridor by turning to **97**.

117

The gale dies away during the night and dawn arrives calm and still. On the horizon to the far north, you can see Ikaya, the ice fortress. The huge crystal-towered stronghold is a wondrous sight, made all the more marvellous because it appears to hover upside down upon a large cloud. 'Kalte mirage,' says Dyce. 'There's no dust in the air here – the land is reflected

in the clouds. That's Ikaya, but the real fortress is over the horizon. It cannot be more than forty miles away now.' Dyce grabs a spade and starts to dig out the Kanu-dogs that have been buried by snow. You wake the others and eat a Meal before setting off once more.

It is midday when you reach the edge of a deep gorge. It is over forty feet wide, and there appears to be no way of crossing it. You are forced to travel along the gorge to the east. Eventually, after three miles, you discover a narrow ice bridge. However, the centre of the bridge is frighteningly thin and narrow: it looks incapable of supporting the weight of a loaded sledge.

You can now see the real Ikaya upon the horizon.

If you wish to risk taking the sledge across the ice bridge, turn to **73**.

If you wish to unload the sledge and ferry the equipment across piece by piece, turn to **162**.

If you decide to leave the sledge here and continue on foot, turn to **223**.

118

He is frail and weak, far too weak to climb. You tell him to tie the rope around his waist so that you can haul him out of the prison. Slowly he follows your instructions. As you draw him up, you are shocked to discover that he weighs no more than a child. You quickly pull him to the comparative safety of the passage. Now you must find out who he is.

Turn to **56**.

119

Great chunks of ice are falling away from the underside of the bridge, and a wide split appears. You manage to keep the sledge on course and reach the far side of the gorge, but you soon discover that a sledge runner is broken and irreparable. You are forced to abandon the sledge and continue on foot, but it still contains some useful equipment. Some of this you may take and store in your Backpack (remembering your maximum of eight Items in total):

> Enough food for up to 5 Meals
> (each counts as 1 Item)
> Sleeping Furs (counts as 2 Items)
> Tent (counts as 3 Items)
> Rope (counts as 2 items)

Fenor, Irian and Dyce quickly follow you across, but as they reach the centre of the bridge, disaster strikes. Dyce catches his foot in the cracked surface and trips. You watch in horror as he slips over the edge. But he catches the edge and hangs on by his fingertips.

'Help me, help me!' he cries, slowly losing his grip.

If you want to try to rescue Dyce, turn to **19**.
If you feel it is too dangerous to try to rescue him, turn to **257**.

120

The raging wind tears at your clothes, and bombards you with sharp flumes of ice and rock. As you raise the Sommerswerd, an intense howling fills your ears. It is a cry of horror and desperation. You strike at the core of this demon, slicing through the cyclone and into the fabric of its being. In an instant, the wind and the ghastly wailing cease – all that remains are the shattered pieces of a hollow statue scattered on the floor.

If you wish to search the altar and alcove of this temple, turn to **274**.

If you wish to leave, you may exit via the northern archway. Turn to **306**.

You are on the very brink of losing your concentration when the rope around your foot loosens and drops away. You dive from the sledge barely seconds before it crashes into the crevasse. The dreadful cries of the Kanu-dogs can be heard as they plummet hundreds of feet into the darkness. Quickly, Fenor runs to your side and drags you away from the crumbling ice edge. You have lost your dog team, your sledge and most of your food, but at least you are still alive.

You and Fenor jump the widening gap and join the rest of your party. After much discussion, the guides agree to continue with the mission even though the hardships will now be doubly severe. In the distance, you see a narrow passage at the edge of the ice shelf where it meets the Hrod Basin. By nightfall, you reach the shelter of this icy pass and camp there for the night. A quick check of your remaining food reveals the need to cut rations by half if all of you are to reach Ikaya. You lose 1 ENDURANCE point due to the poor evening Meal.

Turn to **325**.

Loi-Kymar hands you some strips of cloth with which to plug your nostrils. You take a deep breath, pick up the bowl of smoking herbs and leave the kitchen. Using your Kai Discipline of Camouflage to blend in with the shadows of the corridor, you edge your way nearer and nearer to the unsuspecting guards. You leave the bowl in the shadow of a pilaster and return to the kitchen to wait for it to take effect.

In less than a minute, the Ice Barbarians collapse to the floor and you approach the Hall of the Brumalmarc undetected. You are delighted to discover that one of the great jewelled doors is unlocked. Preparing yourself for attack, you gently push the door ajar and enter Vonotar's chamber.

Turn to **173**.

123

The beast is upon you, its long, barbed, venomous tongue darting at you. You must fight it to the death.

Kalkoth: COMBAT SKILL 11   ENDURANCE 30

If you lose any ENDURANCE points at all during this combat, turn immediately to **66**.

If you win the combat without losing any ENDURANCE points, turn to **174**.

124

You can sense an alien life-force somewhere on the other side of the archway. Concentrating your skill, you try to determine whether it is good or evil. You focus your mental powers until you are almost in a trance, but it is no good – you cannot identify it. At least you have been forewarned by your Kai Discipline of some presence and you prepare yourself to enter the misty arch.

Turn to **264**.

125 – *Illustration VIII*

After two hours of carefully exploring the passage, you are aware that it has gradually descended over two hundred feet. You eventually reach a vast ice vault, the centre of which is filled with a lake. The frozen surface is very thin, and the water beneath it looks dark and deep. You kneel at the edge of the lake, peering into its mysterious depths. Suddenly you see a large black shape pass close to the surface. There is something alive beneath the ice – and it is enormous. Then behind you, you hear the growls of a Kalkoth. The noise is coming from the tunnel. There is only one other exit from this vault which is on the other side of the frozen lake.

If you wish to run across the surface of the lake, turn to **322**.

If you wish to stand and fight the Kalkoth, turn to **207**.

If you have the Kai Discipline of Camouflage, turn to **96**.

126

You notice that the ceiling and walls of the corridor are covered with strange carvings. They seem to depict small cyclones or tornadoes, gradually changing shape into almost human form. Although puzzled by the strange hieroglyphs, you continue until you reach a point where the tunnel takes a sharp right

VIII. Suddenly you see a large black shape pass close to the surface of the ice-lake turn. Only a few feet along the northern wall is another stone door. The lever in the wall next to it is raised and the door is firmly closed. Several yards further ahead, a flight of steps disappears upwards.

If you wish to investigate the door, turn to **246**.
If you wish to continue up the stairs, turn to **323**.

127

You sense that this Helmet has magical properties that can aid you in combat. You detect no evil surrounding this Item or the stone chest in which it lies.

If you wish to take this Helmet and put it on, turn to **308**.

If you are still suspicious of its possible ill effects, leave it untouched and explore the stairs by turning to **323**.

128

As the stone door grinds open, the man jerks his head back in surprise. 'Who's there?' he whispers, in a thin, strangled voice. His eyes glint from beneath the shadow of his ragged hood. Suddenly he seems to recognize you and jumps excitedly to his feet.

'The Gods be praised, a Kai Lord! My name is Tygon. I'm a merchant from Ragadorn. The Ice Barbarians kidnapped me in Ljuk and brought me here. I now await an audience with their new Brumalmarc, the Sommlending sorcerer they call Vonotar: it seems that he shall decide my fate. But if you free me from this sorcerer's pentagram, I'll aid you as best I can.'

You recognize the pentagram to be a circle of binding, a magical prison that can only be broken from the outside. You can easily wipe away part of the circle and free this man.

> If you wish to free him, turn to **170**.
> If you have ever visited Ragadorn, you can ask him some simple questions about the city, to allay any suspicions you may have about who he claims to be, by turning to **11**.
> If you prefer to close the cell door and return to the main corridor, turn to **254**.

129

The barb of the Kalkoth's tongue holds a powerful venom with which it paralyses its victims before eating them. It takes less than five seconds to affect you and you are unconscious before your head hits the snow.

When you awake, you feel something heavy pressing down on your chest. It is the corpse of Irian. As you struggle to your feet, a bleak sight greets you through the early morning mist. Your guides are all dead and the remains of your equipment is scattered across the ledge. The bodies of two Kalkoth lie in the blood-stained snow; both have died from sword wounds. Numbed by cold and shock, you stagger about for nearly an hour searching for your Backpack, before you realize you are still wearing it.

Although still shocked you eventually discover a steep path that leads away from the ledge. The winds of these hostile mountains are bitterly cold. If you have not applied Baknar oil to your skin, you lose 3 ENDURANCE points.

Turn to **155**.

130

You run back past the junction and along the east passage. An Ice Barbarian warrior blocks your path, but you run straight at him. With a bone-jarring thud, you shoulder him aside and keep on running until you reach a staircase. You are halfway up the stairs when you hear the eerie screams of your unnatural pursuers. At the top of the stairs, a corridor runs north to south.

If you wish to go north, turn to **198**.
If you wish to head south, turn to **69**.

131

You sense that these buttons are an ancient lock of some kind. If pressed in the correct order, they may reveal a secret compartment or chamber. But there is also the possibility that, if pressed in the wrong order, they may activate a trap.

If you wish to press the buttons, turn to **227**.
If you do not wish to take the risk of setting off a trap, you can leave the temple by turning to **306**.

132

Unless you have just eaten a Meal, you lose 3 ENDURANCE points from hunger. You continue along the tunnel for over a mile, but you soon become tired and stop to sleep. You awake feeling refreshed, but have no idea just how long you have been sleeping –

the light of these caverns never changes, be it day or night.

You continue onwards, mile after mile, passing through a series of huge ice halls containing towering pillars of crystal. In one vast chamber, you are mesmerized by the beautiful sight of a shimmering crystal ceiling. But beyond this chamber lies an even greater spectacle. A narrow passage leads on to a ledge running around the brink of a huge chasm, over half a mile wide. As you edge your way around this awesome void, you try not to look down into its windswept depths, many miles below.

You have been on the ledge for only a few minutes when a noise behind you makes you glance back. To your horror, you see you are being followed by a monstrous, two-headed serpent.

If you have the Kai Discipline of either Tracking or Animal Kinship, turn to **229**.
If you do not have these skills, turn to **88**.

133

A M'lare bowl hangs from the ceiling directly above the fissure.

If you wish to try to attach your rope to the bowl and swing across, turn to **201**.

(contd over)

If you do not wish to risk falling into the fissure, return along the passage and take the other route by turning to **297**.

134

The following morning, you awake at dawn to the welcome sight of Fenor preparing a hot breakfast. He passes you a steaming bowl, and you gratefully eat its contents. Then you begin loading the equipment on to the sledges for today's journey.

It is a beautiful morning. The wind has dropped and the air is fresh and clear. The Kanu-dogs are strong and eager to be off, and for most of the day the ice is smooth and the running easy. By nightfall, you have reached Syem Island, a pinnacle of granite rising through the ice shelf to a height of four hundred feet. You make camp to the leeward side of the island in order to avoid the worst of the night winds.

Pick a number from the *Random Number Table*.

If the number you have picked is *0–3*, turn to **57**.
If the number you have picked is 4–6, turn to **188**.
If the number you have picked is 7–9, turn to **331**.

135

The Disc fits and the door opens. As you pass through, it quickly slides shut behind you.

You find yourself in a short corridor leading to a curtained arch. Carefully, you part the curtains and peer into a large chamber. You are wise to be so cautious. Standing less than ten feet away is Vonotar the Traitor. In front of him are two Ice Barbarians and he is placing gold bracelets on their wrists. As the doorway behind you is now sealed, it seems you have no alternative but to launch a surprise attack and attempt to capture Vonotar. Steeling yourself, you charge.

Turn to **100**.

136

Suddenly, you are hurled backwards as the ice bridge begins to fall apart. For a few seconds, the sledge balances like a see-saw on the brink; you hear the terrified screams of your guides who are unable to reach you. Their voices are the last sound you will ever hear before the edge of the chasm crumbles away. In a tumble of snow and equipment, you fall to your death two thousand feet below.

Your life and your mission end here.

137

The door grinds open and you enter, ready for attack. You have killed two of the sleeping beasts before the Ice Barbarian and the remaining Doomwolf have time to react. But they both dive at you simultaneously, and you must fight them as one enemy. They are partially immune to Mindblast. If you possess this discipline, add only 1 point to your COMBAT SKILL for the duration of this fight.

Ice Barbarian + Doomwolf:
COMBAT SKILL 30   ENDURANCE 30

If you win the combat, turn to **28**.

138

You have surprised the Kalkoth, and manage to kill one of them before they can turn and fight back. The remaining two beasts attack one at a time, trying to sting you with their barbed tongues.

Kalkoth 1: COMBAT SKILL 11   ENDURANCE 35
Kalkoth 2: COMBAT SKILL 10   ENDURANCE 32

If you lose any ENDURANCE points during this combat, turn immediately to **66**.

If you win the combat without losing any ENDURANCE points, turn to **25**.

You may evade the fight by turning to **277**.

139

You are suddenly aware of a dull throbbing pain in your side. The skin beneath the pocket in which you placed the Glowing Gem is now raw and swollen. You feel dizzy and nauseous, and you are having great difficulty in standing.

If you possess a Red Potion of Laumspur, turn to **116**.

If you do not possess this Potion, turn to **239**.

140

He pulls a hidden bone knife and slashes the back of your hand. You lose 2 ENDURANCE points and drop the struggling child. The boy quickly runs off towards his father, who has now regained his senses and is unsheathing a vicious, tooth-encrusted sword of bone.

Turn to **68**.

141

The man pauses for a few seconds and then answers, 'Killean the Overlord.'

If you now wish to wipe away the pentagram and free him, turn to **170**.

If you do not wish to free him, close the cell door and return to the main corridor by turning to **254**.

142

As you strike it, the mineral splinters into hundreds of silver shards. The rock begins to crack open but the Kalkoth are nearly upon you.

Pick a number from the *Random Number Table*.

If the number you have picked is *0–5*, the overhanging rock collapses and seals off the cave. You can now make your way back to the other tunnel by turning to **284**.

If the number you have picked is *6–9*, the rock does not fall and you must fight the Kalkoth. Turn to **32**.

143

The cone of frost tears through the vines, freezing them instantly. They become brittle and begin to collapse under your weight. You try to leap to safety but it is too late, for the bridge falls away and you are thrown head first into the moat. The last thing you see is Vonotar's evil sneer as he points his crystal rod at your head.

Your mission and your life end here.

144

You plummet into the darkness and crash into an ice ledge over one hundred feet below. Your spine is shattered and you are dead long before your body finally comes to rest in the soft snow on the floor of the crevasse.

Your life and your mission end here.

145 – *Illustration IX*

The passage is short and you quickly arrive at another stone chamber. Ahead you can see a flight of stone stairs leading to a darkened archway high above. At the foot of the stairs, still upright and in armour, are the skeletal remains of an ancient tomb keeper. A large black sword rests in the skeleton's bony fingers.

If you wish to ignore the skeleton and climb the stairs, turn to **36**.

If you wish to attack the skeleton, turn to **278**.

146

You gingerly inch your way back to the rear of the sledge – but you hear the cracking of ice as the crevasse opens wider and wider. 'Jump!' shouts Fenor, as the sledge topples into the widening void.

You steady yourself to try to leap to safety but your left foot becomes entangled in the ropes and equipment.

If you possess the Sommerswerd, turn to **43**.

If you have the Kai Discipline of Mind Over Matter, turn to **121**.

If you possess neither of the above, pick a number from the *Random Number Table*.

(contd over)

IX. At the foot of the stairs, still upright and in armour, are the skeletal remains of an ancient tomb keeper

If the number you have picked is 1–4, turn to **226**.
If the number is 5–9, turn to **266**.
If the number is 0, turn to **312**.

147

You search every square inch of the door and surrounding wall, but there appear to be no unusual features. You are examining the stone ramp when a loud roar freezes your blood. A Kalkoth has entered the ice hall. You turn to see the creature bounding towards you – its jaws are wide open, revealing its barbed tongue. You cannot evade the Kalkoth and you must fight it to the death.

Kalkoth: COMBAT SKILL 10   ENDURANCE 28

If you lose any ENDURANCE points during the course of the combat, turn immediately to **66**.

If you win the combat without losing any ENDURANCE points, turn to **84**.

148

You are halfway down the staircase when you run straight into a patrol of Ice Barbarians. You attempt to fight your way past them, but they are heavily armoured and equipped with swords and spears. You slay many of them before you are surrounded and suffer your death blow.

Your life and your mission end here.

149

You skilfully sidestep as the Ice Barbarian scout stabs at you with a bone-tipped lance.

Pick a number from the *Random Number Table* to see if you have avoided his blow. If you have the Kai Disciplines of Tracking, Hunting or Sixth Sense, you may add 2 to the number that you have chosen.

If your total is now *0–4*, turn to **286**.
If your total is now *5–11*, turn to **333**.

150 – *Illustration X (overleaf)*

Your blow splinters the smooth white surface of the statue. A freezing blast of wind hisses from the crack and, within seconds, a film of glistening ice covers every inch of the chamber. Unless you have applied Baknar oil to your skin, you lose 2 ENDURANCE points due to the sudden drop in temperature.

To your mounting horror, you see that the wind is taking the shape of a small cyclone. It is drawing all the loose ice and rock of the chamber towards its core. You have released an Ice Demon and it is intent on your destruction.

X.   You have released an Ice Demon and it is intent on your
destruction

If you possess the Sommerswerd, turn immediately to **120**.

If you wish to attack the swirling cyclone with a weapon, turn to **18**.

If you wish to try to escape into the distant archway, turn to **211**.

If you possess a Firesphere, turn to **310**.

151

As the hideous beast dies at your feet, you hear Dyce shouting: 'Quick, we've got to get away from here. Kalkoth never hunt alone.'

Grabbing your Backpack, you follow Dyce and Irian along a steep mountain path, up and away from the ice ledge. But you have covered less than fifty yards when disaster strikes. Blinded by the darkness and icy wind, Dyce fails to see that the path comes to an abrupt end at the edge of a sheer precipice. You freeze in horror as you hear your guide's screams fading into the darkness ahead. With death threatening from every side, you cling in desperation to the frozen rockface.

If you have applied Baknar oil to your skin, turn to **209**.

If you have not, turn to **339**.

152

You decide to distract his attention by throwing some Gold Crowns into an alcove directly opposite to him.

Firstly, write down the number of Gold Crowns you are going to throw. Now pick a number from the *Random Number Table*. (0 = 10)

If the number you have picked is equal to or less than the number that you have written down, turn to **319**.

If the number you pick is greater than the number that you have written down, turn to **181**.

153

You are nearly across the lake when catastrophe befalls you. Your right foot crashes through the ice and holds you fast at the knee. You fight to free your leg but it is no good; it is completely trapped. A few seconds later, there is a tremendous crack of splintering ice as the lake monster breaks through to the surface. In terror you see the razor-sharp teeth and black slimy head of the ancient horror bearing down on you. This is the last thing you see before it swallows you whole.

Your life and your mission end here.

154

You are bleeding very badly from a wound in your right leg. It seems as if the flow of blood will never stop, so you tie a makeshift tourniquet around your thigh. You stagger to your feet and survey the damaged chamber.

The monolith must have been designed to guard against or ensnare trespassers. A powerful glyph, which is a spell of explosive power, was obviously placed on it long ago.

You notice a panel in the north wall has opened to reveal a darkened exit from this chamber.

If you wish to explore this new exit, turn to **145**.
If you wish to try to open the door by which you
   entered, turn to **242**.

155

The dawn mists are quickly cleared by the icy mountain wind. Tired, shocked and frozen to the bone, you
claw your way up the cruel rock face until you finally
reach the safety of a wide ridge. You are very hungry
and must eat a Meal here before you continue or lose
3 ENDURANCE points. Remember to subtract the Meal
from your *Action Chart*.

The ridge joins another which you struggle across,
only to find yourself at the top of a terrifying descent.
To reach the narrow mountain pass one thousand
feet below, you must go down a steep and perilous
ice staircase.

Pick a number from the *Random Number Table*. If
your current ENDURANCE point total is less than 10,
deduct 2 from the number that you have picked. If
your current ENDURANCE point total is greater than 20,
add 1 to the number that you have picked.

If your total is now −2–2, turn to **248**.
If your total is now 3–10, turn to **191**.

156

You recognize the aroma of concentrated Gallowbrush, or 'Sleeptooth' as it is commonly called in
Sommerlund. This is the thorny briar your Kai
masters once used to induce sleep when tending to ill
or injured horses. This distilled brew made from the
plant is a very powerful sleeping Potion. If you wish to

keep the Potion, remember to mark it on your *Action Chart* as a Backpack Item.

Now return to **10** and choose your next course of action.

157

You take the Potion from your Backpack and carefully open the door just wide enough to be able to empty the contents of the vial into the bubbling cauldron. You do not have to wait long for the Ice Barbarians to fall asleep after their meal.

The kitchen is small and surprisingly well stocked with herbs. 'These are from the Trading Post at Ljuk,' says Loi-Kymar, peering closely at the labelled jars, several of which he crams into his pockets. Opening two herb jars, he mixes the contents, and offers them to you. 'It will give you strength, Lone Wolf,' he says. You eat the dry leaves and feel a warm glow radiating throughout your body.

Restore 6 ENDURANCE points to your current total, and turn to **301**.

158

As the Ice Barbarian scout is on skis, you will only be able to fight one round of combat before the momentum of his attack carries him past you.

Ice Barbarian Scout: COMBAT SKILL 20   ENDURANCE 28

> If you sustain a higher ENDURANCE point loss than the enemy in this one round of combat, turn to **165**.
>
> If the Ice Barbarian scout loses more ENDURANCE points than you in this one round of combat, turn to **271**.
>
> If you both lose exactly the same number of ENDURANCE points in this one round of combat, turn to **337**.

159

The man stares you straight in the eye and says, 'The Ragad.'

> If you now wish to wipe away the pentagram and free him, turn to **170**.
>
> If you do not want to free him now, close the cell door and return to the main corridor by turning to **254**.

160

Your transport to Ikaya consists of two sledges, each drawn by a team of six Kanu-dogs. This sturdy breed are native to Kalte and make ideal sledge dogs. Their thick tawny coats and powerful chests, as well as their vigour and enthusiasm even in the coldest climates, make them well suited to the work ahead.

On board each sledge is enough food and equipment

for the mission. Your three guides, Irian, Fenor and Dyce, are all experienced trappers. They are skilled at survival in the icy desert, and know of the many unseen dangers.

Once the dogs are harnessed, you and Dyce climb aboard your sledge and signal to the others to lead the way. As you stare across the frozen expanse of the Ljuk ice shelf, you can see a white glare on the distant horizon. This is the Viad Glacier wall, the point where the flow of ice meets the frozen sea. Through the crisp, clear air of Kalte it looks no more than six miles away at most, but in reality it is nearer sixty miles away.

You make good progress on the first day and as darkness approaches, you decide to set up camp for the night. You halt inside a circle of ice pillars that have been forced upwards by the constantly moving ice shelf. The sledges are drawn together and the tent is erected beside them. Once the canvas is secured and the Kanu-dogs have been settled for the night, you begin to prepare your evening meal. Suddenly, a terrifying roar is heard outside the tent.

'By the gods!' cries Irian. 'A Baknar!'

Baknar are large carnivorous creatures that dwell near the Kalte coastline. Their usual prey are Gallings or the smaller Ostrels that live at the sea's edge. But this Baknar has been attracted by the scent of the dogs. It is about to attack and eat several of your sledge dog team.

If you wish to leave the tent and attack the Baknar, turn to **78**.

If you have the Kai Discipline of Hunting, turn to **204**.

If you have the Kai Discipline of Animal Kinship, turn to **318**.

161

The Ice Barbarian slowly advances, his white pupilless eyes sending a shiver down your spine. In his right hand, he clutches a bone scimitar. Although it is raised to strike, his movements are stiff and unsteady as if he were attacking against his will. He is immune to Mindblast.

Ice Barbarian: COMBAT SKILL 17   ENDURANCE 29

If you win the combat, turn to **210**.

162

The sledge is unpacked and the equipment is ferried across piece by piece. Everything is going according to plan until the sledge itself is brought over the gorge. Dyce is steering it, taking great pains to keep it in the centre of the narrow bridge, when suddenly the two lead Kanu-dogs slip and fall into the gorge. They hang helplessly in their harnesses, howling and kicking at the air. Dyce frantically pulls on the reins to try and prevent the others from falling as well, but his efforts are in vain. One by one, the other four dogs are pulled from the bridge by the increasing weight of those below.

'Jump, Dyce, jump!' screams Irian, as the last dog plummets into the void. Dyce leaps clear just as the sledge topples into the gorge, but he lands on the narrowest section of ice and loses his footing.

'Help me, help me!' he cries, his fingers clawing at the slippery ice.

If you wish to attempt to save Dyce, turn to **19**.

If you feel there is no way you can save him, turn to **257**.

163

As you lower the lever, a stone door slides across and seals off the rubbish-strewn chamber. When you raise the lever, the stone door slides open once again.

If you wish to enter the room and investigate its contents, turn to **38**.

If you wish to continue along the east passage, turn to **237**.

164

The tentacled horror rises from the moat and attacks you. You glimpse Vonotar raising his black staff and fixing his gaze towards Loi-Kymar. He is attacking the old magician with his Mindforce. You realize that if Loi-Kymar is killed, the secret of the Guildstaff will die with him.

Before you can do anything else, you must fight the monster to the death. This is an Akraa'Neonor: one of the undead. Remember to double all ENDURANCE points lost by this enemy during the combat, due to the power of the Sommerswerd.

Akraa'Neonor: COMBAT SKILL 23   ENDURANCE 50

If you win the combat in five rounds or less, turn to **272**.

If the combat takes longer than five rounds, turn to **324**.

165

The shock of his attack has knocked you to the ground. By the time you have staggered to your feet, you see that he has stopped and removed his skis.

Turn to **68**.

166

At the bottom of the staircase you discover a new tunnel going northwards. You are about to follow it when your hand touches a lever protruding from the wall to your right. A closer examination reveals a secret door.

If you wish to open the door, turn to **111**.

If you wish to continue along the new tunnel, turn to **336**.

167

The gale gradually drops, the air clears, and the Viad Glacier is revealed in all its splendour. The even surface of ice crystals look like a carpet of snow glittering with gems of every hue – yellow, violet, blue, green, orange and crimson; yet the crystals are of such brilliance, they would put any jewel in the shade. The ice wall rises over eight hundred feet and for the main part it is a smooth but very steep climb. Although the weather is fine, it takes the best part of a day to climb the glacier's edge. All of the equipment has to be unloaded and taken to the top of the glacier where it is repacked on to the sledges. The Kanudogs do hardly anything but fight, and your food is so shaken up in the climb that a gruesome mush is all that remains of it.

By the end you are exhausted. With daylight fading fast, you decide to pitch camp in the shelter of a natural ice bowl, and settle down to a much deserved night's rest.

Pick a number from the *Random Number Table*.

If the number you have picked is *0–6*, turn to **85**.
If the number you have picked is *7–9*, turn to **300**.

168

As you step on to the quartz, you sense a vibration that runs up your leg to your knee. You see that, within the flagstone, a dull light pulsates and a humming sound can be heard emanating from the altar.

With your heart pounding, you prepare yourself for an attack and slowly advance.

Turn to **60**.

169

As you reach the massive door, you desperately cast your eyes over it in the hope of discovering a way to make it open. The door is completely smooth; it has no handle, lock or keyhole. The creature will soon reach the top of the ramp, and you are about to cry out in desperation when you notice a block of granite set into the nearby wall. It has a small triangle cut into its surface.

If you possess a Blue Stone Triangle, turn to **41**.
If you do not, turn to **265**.

170

Using the edge of your cloak, you wipe away a section of the pentagram that is wide enough to let the man escape. You notice that he is painfully thin and unsteady on his feet.

'My thanks Kai Lord. I shall endeavour to repay your kindness some day, if we ever escape from this fortress,' he says. 'You had best lead, for my eyes ail me. I have suffered snow-blindness and the pain still lingers on.'

You lead the way into the passage and are about to turn north into the main corridor, when a pair of steely-fingered hands suddenly close around your throat from behind. A hideous cry betrays the merchant's true identity: he is a Helghast, a deadly shape-changing servant of the Darklords. He has tricked you into releasing him from the pentagram, and he now intends to murder you.

You desperately fight for air as his skeletal fingers burn and tear at your throat. You lose 6 ENDURANCE points. If you are still alive, you manage to break free of his grip, but you must now fight this creature to the death. Due to the surprise of its attack, you cannot swallow any potions before the combat.

If you possess the Sommerswerd, turn to **304**.
If you do not, turn to **175**.

171

The stopper in this Vial is jammed and you have to take great care not to break the slender glass neck. It gradually loosens and you sniff the orange liquid.

If you have the Kai Discipline of either Sixth Sense or Weaponskill, turn to **311**.

If you do not possess either discipline, you become suspicious of this potion and decide to discard it. Return to **10** and decide your next course of action.

172

You decline Irian's offer and return to the tent. However, the others, having congratulated you, leave the tent and join Irian. You watch in amazement as they, too, grab handfuls of Baknar oil and smear it inside their clothing.

Later that night, you eventually get to sleep but only after plugging both nostrils with cloth. The others seem oblivious to the dreadful smell.

Turn to **134**.

173 – *Illustration XI*

The Hall of the Brumalmarc is a vast chamber constructed of crystal blocks rising to a central plateau. On this stands the Brumalmarc throne, as old as Ikaya itself. There, Vonotar sits, surrounded by the tomes and eldritch trappings of a necromancer. He is wrapped in study and does not see you enter the hall.

XI. From out of the dark slithers a huge ghoulish green monster
over which Vonotar has control

He remains oblivious to your presence until Loi-Kymar sneezes.

'Who dares disturb me?' he hisses, rising from the Brumalmarc throne, his eyes searching for an intruder. Upon seeing you, he emits a horrified gasp and fumbles for his black staff. He has the look of a criminal who has been discovered in the act of some dreadful crime. Quickly you raise your weapon and begin to climb the crystal pyramid. You know that you have little time to reach him if you are to over-power and capture him alive.

You reach the edge of the plateau in time to see a wide circle of blocks descending around the throne. Between you and Vonotar, a deep moat is forming. Then from the depths of the moat you hear a ghastly, inhuman gibbering. You brace yourself for combat but are totally unprepared for the horror that now faces you. From out of the dark slithers a huge, ghoulish, green monster. Its deformed head is a mass of tentacles and suckers that ooze a putrid black slime. At the centre of this writhing mass a hideous yellow eye pulsates. Vonotar has control over this monster and he is directing it towards you.

If you possess an Effigy, turn immediately to **34**.
If you do not possess an Effigy but do possess the Sommerswerd, turn to **164**.
If you have neither of the above, turn to **200**.

174

The Kalkoth is dead but its growls still seem to echo around the cavern. You suddenly realize that another of the beasts is now thundering down the tunnel towards you. It is the Kalkoth's mate, and she is hell-bent on revenge. You now have only one possible escape route: you must cross the lake.

Turn to **322**.

175

You sidestep the hissing creature and strike a blow at its head that would maim any mortal warrior. To your horror, the Helghast advances towards you unscathed. It is a powerful captain of the undead, and is immune to normal weapons. An agent of the Darklords, it has been sent to kill Vonotar for his failure at the Battle of Holmgulf. Now free from the pentagram that imprisoned it, the Helghast can complete its mission and return to the rewards and praise of its masters.

You cry out in terror as the Helghast's fingers rend and burn at your throat. But your cries fade unheeded in the dark passage; only death will end your agony.

Your life and your mission end here.

176

Running for the tunnel entrance, you quickly leave the icy river far behind. You follow the tunnel for countless hours as it wends its way northwards. It becomes impossible to recall what hour of the day it is; the perpetual half-light of these caverns never changes. Through fissures in the wall of the tunnel, you catch glimpses of other chambers, and you marvel at the sheer scale of the labyrinth.

You are nearly asleep on your feet when you suddenly detect the aroma of cooked meat. It is coming from a chamber just a few yards ahead to your right. You are very hungry and must soon eat a Meal.

If you wish to investigate the chamber, turn to **5**.
If you wish to ignore the chamber and continue, turn to **132**.

177

You recognize the pungent smell of distilled Grave-weed. This black concentration is a very powerful poison, and you quickly replace the stopper to prevent the noxious fumes from escaping. If you wish to keep this Potion, mark it on your *Action Chart* as a Backpack Item.

Now return to **10** and choose your next course of action.

178

You have been following the Ice Barbarian scouts for nearly two hours when a fierce ice squall rises from the west. The terrain becomes very broken with drifts of snow hiding the razor-sharp ridges and undulations of the ice beneath. For the Ice Barbarian scouts with their skis (fashioned from the ribs of Kalte mammoths), the treacherous surface presents no problems. But to cross it on foot is a slow and painful ordeal.

The biting wind whips across the glacier, bringing with it clouds of fine snow that obscure your vision. You realize the danger of being caught in the open in the middle of a Kalte blizzard, and signal to the others to call off the chase. Walking towards your scouts, you suddenly plummet through the surface of the ice.

Turn to **105**.

179

A bold plan springs to your mind. If you pose as an Ice Barbarian, you may be able to place the bowl of herbs near to the guards; in the dim light of the corridor, the smoke would be difficult to detect. Loi-Kymar agrees to your suggestion and prepares a mixture of herbs to prevent you succumbing to the fumes yourself.

Clad in the furs of an Ice Barbarian, you march along the corridor with the bowl hidden inside your jacket.

Pick a number from the *Random Number Table*.

If the number you have picked is *0–4*, turn to **39**.
If the number you have picked is *5–9*, turn to **296**.

180

Through the snow-swept gloom you can make out two small pinpoints of red light. They are growing larger. Suddenly, in the gloom you see the shape of a large and hideous, four-legged creature. It leaps at you, its red eyes glowering and its fanged mouth open to reveal a long barbed tongue, lashing towards your face.

'Agh! A Kalkoth!' screams Fenor. He rushes to your side, holding a sword high in his hand. He attempts to strike at the creature's tongue. But the creature is already upon you, and you must fight it.

In spite of Fenor's attack the beast only seems to be interested in you. Fenor does not receive any wounds as he stabs at it from behind.

Deduct an additional 3 ENDURANCE points from the Kalkoth's ENDURANCE point total for each round of combat you fight. This represents the damage inflicted by Fenor.

Kalkoth: COMBAT SKILL 11   ENDURANCE 35

- If you kill the creature without losing any ENDURANCE points, turn to **70**.
- If you lose any ENDURANCE points during this combat, turn immediately to **129**.

181

The Gold Crowns clatter along the corridor, but do not have the desired effect. The Ice Barbarian remains at his post, seemingly unaware of the gold now lying just a few feet away.

- If you wish to attempt this ploy again, return to **152**.
- If you have no more Gold Crowns or do not wish to attempt this ploy again, you can attack the guard by turning to **208**.
- If you prefer, you can go back along the corridor, past the junction, and explore the west corridor by turning to **189**.

182

You discover a low passage that opens out into a cavern full of stalagmites. There are two exits in the opposite ice-wall; both disappear into darkness. In the snow around the entrances of both tunnels are many strange tracks.

If you have the Kai Discipline of Tracking, turn to **75**.

If you wish to take the right tunnel, turn to **114**.

If you wish to explore the left tunnel, turn to **235**.

183

You sprint towards the northern corridor as fast as your twisted ankle will allow.

Pick a number from the *Random Number Table*. If you have the Kai Discipline of Hunting, add 2 to the number you have picked.

If your total is now *0–3*, turn to **89**.

If your total is now *4–11*, turn to **215**.

184

The tunnel is short and soon leads you to a small cavern. In the centre of the cavern lie two corpses, both human. In spite of the freezing temperature, they are badly decomposed; they have obviously

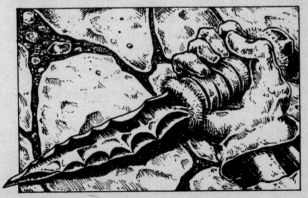

been dead for a very long time. Both are attired in furs and one still has a flint dagger grasped in his hand. From the position of the bodies, it looks as if they killed each other in a desperate fight.

If you wish to search the corpses, turn to **298**.

If you wish to continue, you may leave this cavern by the tunnel in the far wall. Turn to **315**.

If you wish to retrace your steps and take the other tunnel, turn to **125**.

185

You focus your power upon the lock, but you find it difficult to visualize the inner mechanism.

Pick a number from the *Random Number Table*. If you have the Kai Discipline of Sixth Sense, you may add 2 to this number.

If your total is now *0–4*, turn to **22**.

If your total is now *5–11*, turn to **326**.

186

The dead Ice Barbarian's child cowers over his father's body and stares at you with hatred blazing in his eyes. You notice that the other Ice Barbarian scouts are closing in and you must act quickly to save yourself.

You decide to use the boy as a hostage, but he is like a wild animal. He bites, scratches and kicks to free himself from your grip.

Turn to **320**.

187

As you close the Bracelet around your wrist, a terrible pain shoots through your head. You are being attacked by a powerful Mindforce, which is draining your will.

If you have the Kai Discipline of Mindshield, turn immediately to **258**.

If you do not possess this skill, turn to **93**.

188

The next day, thick snow clouds have descended over the Ljuk ice shelf and there is little wind. As you draw closer to the edge of the glacier, the surface of the ice shelf becomes very rough and broken. Slabs of solid ice jut out at every angle, forming difficult obstacles. You are forced to dismount from the sledges and manhandle them across the hummocks and ridges, as you try to reach the smoother slope of the distant Viad Glacier.

You have covered half a mile when ahead you see a large crevasse. This great crack in the ice is only two or three feet wide; but it extends for over a mile in either direction. For safety's sake, you agree to tie a rope around your waists and link up together. Should one person fall into a crevasse, the others should be able to pull him out.

You cross this narrow fissure successfully, only to find yourselves in a maze of crevasses. Thin layers of snow hide their locations, and you only detect their presence by testing the ground with your weapon.

You have covered less than half a mile when you come to a crevasse over eight feet wide. You stare downwards, but there is no light to be seen in the black yawning void. Your sledges are ten feet long and could bridge the gap. But if the icy edge were to collapse, you could lose all your equipment at once.

> If you wish to unload the sledges and use them as a bridge, turn to **232**.
>
> If you wish to jump across with the Kanu-dogs, and then pull the sledges after you, turn to **346**.

189

You continue along the corridor for over fifteen minutes until you reach a massive stone doorway, twenty feet high. Placing your ear to the warm surface, you feel the stone vibrating and hear low rumbling noises. Like the other stone doors of Ikaya, this entrance has a lever in the nearby wall.

> If you wish to pull the lever and enter, turn to **292**.
>
> If you do not wish to enter, you can return to the junction and take the east passage by turning to **97**.

190

Letting the boy go free at the last possible moment, you grab the sledge whip and lash the dogs, driving them for everything they are worth. On all sides, flurries of arrows whistle past you and several thud into the framework of the empty sledge. A couple of the Ice Barbarian scouts give chase, but your dog team is now much faster and you soon out distance even their arrows.

By nightfall, you reach the very edge of the Viad Mountains. This vast granite range rises sheer out of the ice and snow and presents you with an impassable barrier on such a moonless night. Meanwhile a wind arises in the west, heralding a night squall. You must find shelter or you will surely perish in the blizzard.

If you have the Kai Discipline of either Tracking or Sixth Sense, turn to **348**.

If you do not have either of these skills, you can look for shelter towards the north by turning to **27**.

If you prefer, you can search towards the south by turning to **314**.

191

Shaking with shock and exhaustion, you finally reach the pass just as night is about to fall. In the distance, you see a small cave located directly beneath a frozen waterfall. The wind has become much stronger and you decide to take shelter in the cave for the night. However as you enter, you are surprised to see a shaft of light falling from a fissure at the rear of the cave.

You cautiously approach the strange glow, but fail to see a snow covered crevasse and fall in a tumble of snow and ice.

Turn to **40**.

192

If you possess a Glowing Crystal, turn to **267**.
If you do not, turn to **44**.

193

You have cuts and bruises on both legs and your nose bleeds from striking it against a stalactite. You lose 2 ENDURANCE points, but you can count yourself very lucky: you narrowly escaped stepping into a deep fissure hidden in the darkness. Make the necessary adjustments to your *Action Chart*.

Turn to **235**.

194

Your skill and patience finally pay off. A subtle *click* indicates you have been successful, and as you remove your blade, the great stone lid slowly opens to reveal a magnificent Silver Helmet.

If you wish to wear this splendid helmet, mark it on your *Action Chart*, and turn to **308**.
If you decide to leave it in the stone chest, you may continue your exploration towards the stairs by turning to **323**.

195

As you leap across to the opposite ledge, a tremor shakes the ice and the crevasse suddenly widens. You slip, hitting your head on the edge as you drop into the gaping void. The cord attaching the safety rope to your belt snaps, and you fall into darkness.

Turn to **21**.

196

The struggle is desperate but in your very desperation you find the strength to survive.

Any weapon(s) you had has been dragged from your grasp and, bombarded by ice and stone, you lose 2 ENDURANCE points. Make the necessary adjustments to your *Action Chart*. However, you manage to crawl to the safety of the northern archway. You are now unarmed but grateful to be alive.

Turn to **306**.

197

You can see another passage leading out of the cavern towards the north.

If you wish to creep past the sleeping creatures towards the tunnel, turn to **125**.

If you do not want to take the risk of waking them, you can return the way you have just come and enter the other tunnel by turning to **235**.

If you wish to attack the sleeping creatures, you can do so by turning to **109**.

198

The corridor ends at a large stone door. Unlike the others, this door has no lever to open it, but you do notice that a small slot has been cut into a nearby wall. You are examining the slot when you are disturbed by a howling mob of mutated Ice Barbarians, advancing along the corridor towards you. You prepare for combat but there are too many of them for you. Although you fight bravely, they eventually overwhelm you and stab you to death.

Your life and your mission end here.

199

After nearly a mile, the ice-walled tunnel opens out into a beautiful grotto. Melt-water cascades over a large outcrop of silvery mineral, which casts a dazzling display of reflections.

You can see that there is a small cave beneath the waterfall, which disappears into the silver rock. There appear to be no other exits from the grotto.

If you wish to enter the cave, turn to **82**.
If you wish to return along the passage and take the other tunnel, turn to **284**.

200

The ghastly tentacled horror rises out of the moat and attacks you. You must fight it to the death.

Akraa'Neonor: COMBAT SKILL 22　ENDURANCE 50

During the combat, you glimpse Vonotar, his black staff raised, fixing his gaze on Loi-Kymar. He is attacking the old man with the force of his mind. If Loi-Kymar is killed, the secret of his Guildstaff will die with him.

If you win the combat in seven rounds or less, turn to **272**.
If the combat lasts more than seven rounds, turn to **324**.

201

The bowl creaks and splinters of stone fall from the ceiling as you swing across the black fissure, but you are lucky; the Rope holds and you land safely on the other side. With a flick of your wrist you retrieve the Rope and set off along the passage.

You have gone only a few yards when you notice an arched stone door to your left, adorned with strange carvings. These carvings depict hundreds of skeletons entwined around smooth blocks of stone. To the side of the door you see that a lever in the wall is raised.

If you wish to pull the lever and open the door, turn to **110**.

If you wish to continue along the passage, turn to **63**.

202

Suddenly the Kalkoth stop roaring. They have picked up the scent of Baknar oil on your skin. Within seconds they appear and charge towards you.

If you wish to stand and fight them, turn to **263**.
If you wish to turn and run, turn to **277**.

203

A small spyhole has been cut into the centre of the door. You cautiously peer through and see the old man in blue robes who you saw before through the portal above the cell.

If you wish to open the door, pull the lever in the nearby wall and turn to **56**.
If you wish to ignore the old man, continue along the corridor towards the junction by turning to **276**.

204

Baknar are fierce and dangerous creatures. They are afraid of only one thing – fire. Grabbing a torch from the pile of equipment, you light it and leave the tent.

The wind has become much stronger since you first made camp. It whips the fine snow into small whirlwinds that sting your eyes. A moving shadow to your right betrays the Baknar as it lopes towards you. It is preparing to pounce when it sees your guttering torch and shrieks in terror. Seconds later, it has disappeared into the darkness. A quick check of the Kanu-dogs reveals that they are all safe, although still understandably nervous. To ensure that the Baknar does not attack again, you all take it in turns to sit watch that evening, torches and weapons at the ready.

Turn to **134**.

205

During the night, a fierce blizzard rages, burying your makeshift shelter in over twelve feet of snow. The cold numbs your hands and feet and slowly drains the strength from your body. You slip into a sleep from which you will never awake, for you suffocate to death beneath the snows of Kalte.

Your mission and your life end here.

206

Holding your equipment and your breath, you try to land as quietly as you can on the dusty floor of the corridor. Unfortunately, you twist your ankle in the fall and cannot stifle a yelp of pain. Lose 1 ENDURANCE point. Then, to your horror, you see an Ice Barbarian seated less than thirty feet away to your left. His head is slowly turning in your direction. However, a quick glance to your right reveals another corridor heading north, less than fifteen feet from where you now kneel.

If you have the Kai Discipline of Camouflage, turn to **74**.

If you do not have this skill, you can try to run for the north corridor and pray that the Ice Barbarian does not see you. Turn to **183**.

If you prefer, you can attack and attempt to silence the Ice Barbarian before he can raise the alarm, by turning to **161**.

207

You can see the shadowy outline of the hideous creature as it charges towards you along the tunnel. It is blind with rage and hungry for blood. You suddenly realize that if you dive aside as the creature leaps from the tunnel, it may just miss you and plunge headlong on to the thin ice of the lake.

If you wish to try to dive aside when the Kalkoth charges from out of the tunnel, turn to **80**.

If you wish to stand and fight it when it appears, turn to **253**.

208

The Ice Barbarian sees you approach and draws his bone sword. He moves to the centre of the bottom stair to prevent you running past him.

Ice Barbarian: COMBAT SKILL 17   ENDURANCE 30

If you win the combat within four rounds, turn to **4**.

If you win the fight in more than four rounds, turn to **81**.

209

All night you cling to the frozen rockface. The icy wind whips you and you shiver uncontrollably as you fight to stay conscious. You lose 2 ENDURANCE points. However, the Baknar oil keeps you from losing all your essential body warmth and on this desperate occasion, it saves your life.

Turn to **155**.

210

A tooth-encrusted Bone Sword lies at the Barbarian's side. You may take this weapon if you wish. You search his body and also discover a Gold Bracelet on his left wrist.

If you have Kai Discipline of Sixth Sense, turn to **316**.

If you wish to take the Gold Bracelet, turn to **236**. (Put it on your wrist and mark it on your *Action Chart* as a Special Item.)

If you do not wish to take the Bracelet, make your way quickly along the corridor towards a distant junction by turning to **215**.

211

The cyclone is tearing at your clothes and bombarding you with chunks of ice and rock. You grit your teeth and try to run but the cold saps your strength, and you are forced to claw your way along the wall to avoid being sucked into the swirling vortex.

Pick a number from the *Random Number Table*. If your current ENDURANCE point total is less than *10*, deduct 3 from the number you have picked.

If your number is now *−3 to 3*, turn to **95**.
If your number is now *4–9*, turn to **196**.

212

When you arrive back at the tent, Dyce cooks a delicious Meal that fills your stomach and raises your spirits. You have made good progress and, in spite of the physical hardships, you feel confident and eager to continue.

Irian fetches the sleeping furs from the sledge and you all prepare for a good night's sleep. The only clothes you ever remove are your boots – the few days that you have spent in this desolate land have taught you much about survival. As you take off your boots, you take care to leave them in the shape of your feet: in these temperatures, your soft boots soon freeze as hard as stone, making them agony to put on next morning if you don't. Unlacing the boots requires bare fingers, and you constantly have to pause and thrust your hands back into your mittens to avoid frostbite setting in. Curled up in your furs, your teeth chattering, and the wind howling outside, you eventually fall into a deep sleep.

Turn to **238**.

213

You point the Sommerswerd towards Vonotar's crystal rod. In an instant, the cone of frost arcs away from the bridge and shatters against the golden sword. You hear Vonotar curse you as, once again, the power of the Sommerswerd saves you from his destructive magic.

Turn to **252**.

214

Unfortunately, the Kalkoth has picked up your scent and launches an attack on your hiding place. Its huge paw swipes at you and claws open the sleeve of your jacket. You lose 2 ENDURANCE points. You realize you can only escape this creature by running across the lake.

If you wish to escape from the Kalkoth, turn to **322**.

If you wish to fight it, turn to **123**.

215

Turning a corner, you breathe a sigh of relief. Behind you all is silent. But you become aware that the low rumbling sound you detected earlier is much louder in this corridor. A few yards along to your left, a short passage leads to a closed stone door.

If you wish to investigate the door, turn to **13**.
If you wish to continue along the corridor towards the north, turn to **254**.

216 – *Illustration XII (overleaf)*

You have covered less than a mile when the first of the Ice Barbarian scouts appear to the north on skis. At first, there are only two of the fearsome warriors, but they are soon joined by three others. They are large, muscular and bedecked with furs. Some of them wear bone armour. Despite their size, they glide across the snow with an almost feline grace and speed. Each of them has a pole attached to his back from which a small flag flutters.

Suddenly, a bone-tipped arrow whistles past your knee and embeds itself in the sledge. An Ice Barbarian scout skis past to your right. He is less than ten yards away and you can clearly see his slanted eyes and sharp cheek-bones. You suddenly realize that what you had mistaken for muscle and fur is in fact an Ice Barbarian child. Each scout is carrying a large backpack containing a small child. These children are armed with small bone bows, and they fire a constant stream of arrows as their fathers ski nearer and nearer.

Suddenly Irian falls, an arrow buried in his back.

XII.   Each Ice Barbarian scout is carrying a backpack containing a child armed with a bone bow

Dyce runs to his aid but is shot down before he has taken a dozen steps. Fenor is hit. An arrow passes straight through his throat. He bravely staggers on for nearly a minute before collapsing in the snow. You are on your own. An Ice Barbarian scout skis past to your left and returns towards you head on. He has a spear under one arm, which is levelled at your chest.

If you wish to fight the Ice Barbarian scout, turn to **158**.

If you wish to try and escape, turn to **149**.

217

The monolith suddenly explodes, sending hundreds of razor-sharp shards screaming through the air. You are pierced by the stone shrapnel and thrown to the far wall by the sheer force of the blast. You lose 10 ENDURANCE points.

If you are still alive, turn to **154**.

218

The bone box contains a beautiful Diamond. Its many facets gleam and sparkle, even in the dim half-light of the ice hall. In Sommerlund, a jewel of this size and quality would be worth thousands of crowns. If you wish to keep the Diamond, slip it into your pocket and mark it on your *Action Chart* as a Special Item.

You can now examine the fortress door by turning to **52**.

219

You sense that the low rumbling noise echoing throughout this part of Ikaya is much louder along the west corridor than the east. There is something unnatural about its tone that makes you feel uneasy. You decide to avoid the west corridor and set off towards the east.

Turn to **349**.

220

The next day is bitterly cold. A strong wind from the west blows relentlessly as you steer your sledge towards the Hrod Basin. The snow clogs your eyes and your lips crack and bleed, but by midday you reach the edge of the basin. Irian and Dyce's sledge arrives at the ice wall first and they eagerly encourage you onwards.

Without any warning, a great crack appears between the two sledges, opening with a tremendous roar, until you are faced by a huge dark crevasse. Frantically you pull on the reins but it is too late to prevent your Kanu-dog team from disappearing into the void. Your sledge is left balancing on the edge of the crevasse, while the team of howling Kanu-dogs dangle helplessly in their harnesses below you. Very carefully, you risk a glance into the chasm. You see that the first two dogs have broken free and dropped over one-hundred-and-fifty feet to a ledge below. One of them appears to be dead. The other is badly injured and whimpers beside the still body of its comrade. Suddenly, a shudder jolts the sledge and you gasp with fright.

If you wish to crawl with Fenor to the rear of the sledge, turn to **146**.

If you decide to try to leap clear of the sledge on to the cracked ice, turn to **29**.

221

The corridor in which you now stand is far warmer than the icy cavern outside. For the first time in many days, you can lower the hood of your cloak and remove your mittens without risking frostbite.

You notice that the stone passage ascends to a landing where another passage branches off to the east. M'lare bowls hang at regular intervals along the arched ceiling, their unnatural light illuminating the carved walls.

As you approach the landing, you notice an archway leading into a small room beyond. A strange sight meets your eyes. Ragged furs, pottery shards and the debris of hundreds of years seem to have been thrown into this chamber. A large lever protrudes from the wall beside the archway.

If you wish to enter the room and investigate the contents, turn to **38**.

If you wish to pull the lever, turn to **163**.

If you wish to explore eastwards along the passage, turn to **237**.

222

Using your Kai skill, you press yourself into the shadow cast by a pilaster. The Ice Barbarians pass within six inches of you, but do not detect that you are there. Once you are sure that they have disappeared, you emerge from the shadows and continue along the corridor.

Turn to **330**.

223

The sledge contains the following equipment. You may take any of the following Items and store them in your Backpack, but remember that your Pack can only hold a maximum of 8 Items:

> Enough Food for 1–5 Meals
> (each Meal counts as 1 Item)
> Tent (counts as 3 items)
> Sleeping Furs (counts as 2 items)
> Long Rope (counts as 2 items)

Dyce volunteers to return to the *Cardonal* with the Kanu-dog teams and the sledge, while the rest of you push on towards Ikaya, the ice fortress.

Ikaya was carved out of the Hrod Range many ages ago, by a race of creatures that have long since disappeared. Thousands of years passed before the Ice Barbarians migrated here from the Uncharted Void, claiming Ikaya for themselves. Their leaders, the 'Brumalmarc' as they are called, have ruled over Kalte from the safe shelter of this fortress ever since.

You have covered nearly five miles when Irian suddenly points to the west. 'There . . . over there. I'm sure I saw something.'

You halt and strain your eyes to try to identify something unusual in the monotonous landscape of ice and snow.

'Look over there!' shouts Fenor, pointing towards a ridge less than a mile away. Two fur-clad warriors are standing on top of a large slab of ice. They are staring at you.

'Ice Barbarians!' whispers Irian, his voice shaking with fear. 'If they beat us to Ikaya, we're as good as dead.'

You are still ten miles from the ice fortress and less than two hours of daylight remain.

> If you wish to ignore the Ice Barbarians and press on to Ikaya, turn to **327**.
>
> If you wish to attack them, and try to prevent them warning others, turn to **307**.

224

Twenty feet directly below the portal, you can see a man dressed in a dark cloak. He is kneeling in the centre of a large pentagram, which is chalked on the floor of the dingy cell.

> If you wish to call to the man, turn to **67**.
>
> If you decide to remain silent, leave the portal and continue on your way along the passage towards the stairs by turning to **166**.

225

The stopper is sealed with wax. If you wish to break the seal, you must risk smashing the thin glass of the Vial.

If you wish to attempt to break the seal, turn to **54**.

If you are suspicious of the contents and do not wish to risk breaking the Vial, leave it and return to **10** to choose your next course of action.

226

You frantically pull at your trapped foot and free it just as the sledge topples over into the crevasse. Fenor rushes to your side and pulls you away from the crumbling edge of this void. You both safely jump the widening gap and join the others.

You have lost your dogs, your sledge and most of your food, but you are alive. In spite of the loss and the additional hardships that will result, your guides agree to continue the mission.

In the distance you can see a narrow passage at the edge of the ice shelf where it joins the Hrod Basin. By nightfall, you have reached the shelter of this narrow pass and decide to set up camp. A quick check of your remaining food soon reveals the need to cut rations by half in order to reach Ikaya. Lose 1 ENDURANCE point due to the meagre evening Meal.

Turn to **325**.

227

The stone buttons rise less than an inch above the smooth altar surface. You notice that they are each surrounded by strange, barely perceptible, hieroglyphs, eroded by the passage of time. You now have to decide in which sequence you will press the buttons. If you possess the Kai Discipline of Mind Over Matter, you can depress the buttons without actually touching them.

If you decide to press the left button then the right, turn to **102**.

If you decide to press the right button, then the left, turn to **334**.

If you decided to press them both together, turn to **299**.

228

You draw on all your powers of concentration to levitate the bowl of fuming herbs, and send it hovering along the corridor. You bring it to rest in the shadow of the pilaster and watch its effects with great curiosity; for in less than a minute, the Ice Barbarian guards have collapsed to the floor.

'Now's our chance,' whispers Loi-Kymar, and he ushers you out of the kitchen. You approach the Hall of the Brumalmarc undetected and discover that one of the magnificent jewelled doors is unlocked. Drawing your weapon, you gently push the door ajar and enter Vonotar's chamber.

Turn to **173**.

229

You recognize the serpent to be a Javek, a two-headed and deadly poisonous ice snake. As it slithers nearer, you can clearly see the open jaw of the second head and the yellow, curved fangs dripping with venom. It moves very quickly and you know that you will not be able to outrun it along this narrow ledge.

If you possess a Firesphere, turn to **46**.

If you do not, you must prepare to fight. Turn to **88**.

230

The Helghast smoulders and decays at your feet, a vile green gas seeping from beneath its robes. As you stare at the remains, you realize that this creature must have been sent here to kill Vonotar by the Darklords who crave Vonotar's death for his failure at the Battle of Holmgulf. The evil wizard must have discovered the Helghast and imprisoned it within a pentagram until he could devise some way of killing it for good.

You gingerly touch your wounded throat and thank the gods that you wield the Sommerswerd – its power has once again saved your life. You turn and quickly descend the stairs, leaving behind the Helghast's foul remains.

Turn to **166**.

231

You sense that something is very wrong here. There are no mines in Kalte, and, as a result, not only gold but all metals are considered rare and precious. The only means by which Ice Barbarians can obtain metal is by fur trading at Ljuk each summer, and then it is only steel that interests them. You suspect therefore, that these bracelets are worn by force rather than choice. If you wish to put on one of the Gold Bracelets, mark it on your *Action Chart* as a Special Item.

If you take a Bracelet, turn to **187**.
If you wish to ignore the Bracelets and continue your exploration of Ikaya, turn to **63**.

232

It takes nearly an hour to cross, but you eventually make it in safety. The ascent of the glacier is a daunting task. The ice wall is smooth but very steep, rising over eight hundred feet. All of the equipment has to be unloaded from the sledges and ferried to the top of the glacier, where it is repacked piece by piece. The Kanu-dogs do hardly anything but fight amongst themselves and your food gets so shaken up, that all that remains to eat that evening is an unsavoury mess.

On the summit of the glacier wall, you pitch tent in the shelter of a natural ice bowl and settle down to a much-deserved rest.

Pick a number from the *Random Number Table*.

If the number you have picked is *0–6*, turn to **85**.
If the number you have picked is *7–9*, turn to **300**.

233

You recognize the liquid to be distilled Laumspur, a herb of great healing properties. This concentrated Potion is powerful enough to restore 5 ENDURANCE points. If you wish to keep this Vial, remember to mark it on your *Action Chart* as a Backpack Item.

(contd over)

Now return to **10** and decide your next course of action.

234

The man hesitates and then answers. 'Why, the Rusty Anchor Inn, of course.'

If you now wish to wipe away the outside of the pentagram and free him, turn to **170**.

If you do not wish to free him, close the cell door and return to the main corridor by turning to **254**.

235 – *Illustration XIII*

After a short walk, you arrive at a massive ice hall full of crystal stalagmites and stalactites. The floor is covered with animal tracks and bones, yet the vast hall seems empty and still. You notice that the northern wall is a completely smooth surface of granite blocks stretching upwards to the icy ceiling, over one hundred feet above. You suddenly realize that you are staring at the foundation stones of Ikaya – you have reached the ice fortress.

Partially obsured by a large mound of crystals, you can just make out a ramp leading up to a massive stone door in the fortress wall. Your discovery brings renewed hope. If you can gain entry to Ikaya and quickly capture Vonotar, there is still time to reach your ship, the *Cardonal*, before the pack ice starts to freeze.

If you wish to cross the icy hall and examine the stone door, turn to **52**.

If you decide to stop and search the bone-littered floor, turn to **115**.

XIII.   You arrive at a massive ice hall full of crystal stalagmites
and stalactites

236

As the Gold Bracelet snaps shut around your wrist, a terrible pain shoots through your head. You are being attacked by a powerful Mindforce, that is trying to drain your will.

If you possess the Kai Discipline of Mindshield, turn immediately to **345**.

If you do not possess this Kai Discipline, turn to **9**.

237

You soon reach the bottom of a flight of broad stone steps that ascends northwards to a landing, thirty feet above. The centre of each step has been worn smooth by the feet of the countless creatures that once inhabited the lower levels of cold Ikaya. As you climb, you wonder how long you will remain undetected. So far you have neither seen nor heard any other living soul in these deserted passages.

You have the element of surprise on your side; you now pray that Vonotar is unprepared for an intruder from the depths of his own fortress. You reach the landing and pass through an empty hall, towards a darkened archway beyond. Here, the passage splits and branches off towards the east and west. You are hungry and must now eat a Meal or lose 3 ENDURANCE points.

If you wish to take the east passage, turn to **92**.

If you decide to take the west passage, turn to **297**.

238

The two days that follow are sheer hell. Ridges formed by deeply fissured ice-mounds continually bar your way, and you are forced to dismount and manhandle the sledges across them. Progress is slow. The Kanu-dogs are nervous and take fright at the slightest instance and the sledges frequently capsize and spill their loads.

A haze of fine snow obscures your vision. On two occasions, Fenor and Irian slip into crevasses and have to be pulled out by their safety ropes. Then your sledge meets with a similar mishap. Dyce volunteers to be lowered into the crevasse on the end of a rope, and unloads the damaged sledge so that it is light enough to be hauled out. After two hours of back-breaking effort, the sledge is dragged from the void, but only for you to discover that it is damaged beyond repair and will have to be abandoned.

A gale rises from the west, and blows so fiercely that you have difficulty in standing. Within a few minutes, the conditions have become so bad that you are obliged to pitch a tent and wait for the gale to die down. Hour after hour, the wind buffets the tent relentlessly. As you slowly drift off to sleep, you can only dread what the next morning may bring; you are totally unaware of the amazing sight that awaits you.

Turn to **117**.

239

You quickly lose consciousness. You have succumbed to the baneful power of an ancient Doomstone, a power that is deadly to all living creatures. Death is inevitable and comes quickly.

It may be of consolation to learn that your body is soon discovered by an Ice Barbarian guard, who presents it (together with the Doomstone) to Vonotar. The traitor is so elated by your death, that he orders your body to be encased in ice and displayed like a trophy in his hall. However, the radiations of the Doomstone will cause the evil wizard months of suffering and eventually bring about his own death.

Your life and your mission end here.

240

You fall over thirty feet and land flat on your back in the snow-filled crevasse. You are surrounded by sharp stalagmites and jagged ice, but you have miraculously escaped death and injury. Shaken, but thankful to be alive, you stagger to your feet and grasp a crystal stalagmite for support. You slowly become aware that you can see your hands quite clearly. A faint light is seeping from a fissure to your left. With curiosity getting the better of your natural caution, you stagger across the crevasse floor and explore this mysterious cave.

Turn to **284**.

241

The Ice Barbarian is on his knees when you enter combat; he cannot react to your attack during the first two rounds. Ignore any ENDURANCE points you lose during the first two rounds of combat.

Ice Barbarian: COMBAT SKILL 18   ENDURANCE 28

If you win the combat, turn to **186**.

242

The stone door is perfectly smooth. No hinges, locks or levers are visible from inside the room.

If you possess the Sommerswerd, turn to **42**.

If you do not possess it, you can only leave this room via the passage in the north wall. Turn to **145**.

243

You are remarkably lucky. Hidden by the darkness is a deep fissure into which you nearly stepped. With a few extra bruises to your knees and shins, you press onwards towards the distant light.

Turn to **235**.

244

You carefully make your way across the temple floor until you are standing next to the altar. The statue seems cold and lifeless, but you sense that someone or something is trapped within. You can almost hear their desperate cries for release.

If you wish to strike the statue with a weapon, turn to **150**.

If you do not possess a weapon, or if you wish to leave the temple, head towards the northern archway by turning to **306**.

245

As the beast shrieks a ghastly death-cry, the horrible stench of its body fills your nostrils. Even the Kanu-dogs wrinkle their noses in disgust and shy away from the evil smell.

When Irian appears at your side with a skinning knife, you wince at the thought of skinning this dreadful creature. You watch with distaste as Irian cuts open the beast from throat to belly, and peels back the thick white fur. You cannot believe your eyes when he scoops out handfuls of thick oil from inside the skin and smears it all over his face and body. 'Baknar oil,' he shouts enthusiastically. 'Keeps you dry and warm. Better than fur for keeping out the Kalte ice.' He offers you a handful of the vile oil.

If you wish to accept his offer, turn to **91**.
If the thought of smelling like a vat of rancid cheese does not appeal to you, turn to **172**.

246

You depress the lever and the stone door slides aside to reveal a large chamber. It is cold, stale and empty, except for a granite chest lying near the east wall.

If you wish to make a closer examination of the chest, turn to **45**.
If you decide to ignore the chamber and continue up the stairs instead, turn to **323**.

247

The old man slowly raises his head. His eyes look tired and bruised. The congealed blood of several wounds matts his long grey beard. He struggles to his feet and peers into the darkness above. 'Who lurks there? Is that you Vonotar? Show yourself, worm, or be gone. I'll not cower from you, nor will I hide my loathing. You will never break me, traitor!' he shouts, defiantly shaking his scrawny fist in the air.

You cannot mistake his accent, for it is identical to your own. The old man is one of your countrymen, a Sommlending from the northern port of Toran.

> If you possess a Rope, you can lower it to the floor and rescue the old man from the cell by turning to **118**.
> If you do not have a Rope, or if you do not wish to rescue him, you can continue along the passage by turning to **30**.

248

About three hundred feet from the base of the ice staircase, you become dizzy and lose your footing. You try desperately to hang on to the rockface, but your fingers are numb with the cold and you fall to your doom in the valley below. The perfectly preserved remains of your body will be found by explorers, two thousand years from now.

Your mission and your life end here.

249

You sense that a group of warriors is approaching from the south.

Take the north corridor by turning to **104**.

250

The glass shatters in your hand, and the black liquid splashes over the stone table. Cursing your misfortune, you carefully sniff the few remaining drops lying in a curve of jagged glass.

If you have ever visited the Graveyard of the Ancients, turn to **77**.

If you have not, you are suspicious of this pungent liquid, and quickly discard the broken glass. Return to **10** and choose your next course of action.

251

In the afternoon, your journey towards the glacier gradually becomes far more laborious. The blood vessels in both your eyes begin to swell until you feel as though your eyeballs are being tatooed with red-hot needles, or as if your eyelids are full of grit and sand.

Fenor is the first to notice your condition, and he halts the sledges. 'Snow-blindness,' he says, tearing an old rag into long strips of bandage. 'If you go on like that, you'll go mad with pain before nightfall.'

You lose 2 ENDURANCE points. Your sore eyes are swathed in bandages and you are made to lie amongst the equipment at the rear of the sledge. Then the trek continues. By nightfall, you reach the edge of the Viad Glacier.

Turn to **62**.

'Your time has come,' shouts a voice, but it is Loi-Kymar and not Vonotar who now speaks. A knot of herbs flies through the air and hits Vonotar squarely in the chest. In an instant, the hunchback wizard is engulfed in a tangle of vines that ensnare him from head to toe. Loi-Kymar bridges the moat with creepers and joins you on the platform.

'Be sure to remove his rings and amulets,' he says, as he busily searches for his Guildstaff. 'He is a master of trickery. We would not want him to miss the special homecoming that awaits him in Sommerlund.'

You marvel at the old man's composure. After such a desperate fight, he seems completely unruffled. 'Ah! Here she is,' he announces triumphantly as he withdraws his Guildstaff from beneath the Brumalmarc throne.

You pass him your map of Kalte and point out the location of the *Cardonal*. 'I'll not be needing that,' he replies, a little contemptuously. 'Maps are invariably wrong – I prefer to rely on my own sense of direction.' The old magician raises his staff and a dazzling beam of light shoots from its tip. He makes three wide sweeps of the air and the Hall of the Brumalmarc is transformed into an umbrella of colour.

Turn to **350**.

253

The Kalkoth hits you with such force that you tumble backwards onto the thin ice of the lake. You are

XIV.   In an instant, the hunchback wizard is engulfed in a tangle of vines concussed, and unconscious of the sharp teeth that now engulf your sinking body.

Your life and your mission end here.

254

On the west wall of the corridor you see another stone door, with a small spyhole cut into the centre revealing a cell on the other side. An old man is huddled in the far corner of the cell, his face and hair matted with blood and dirt. His blue robes are so filthy that the crescents and stars embroidered on them are almost totally obscured.

If you wish to open the cell door, turn to **56**.
If you decide to ignore this old man, and continue along the corridor, turn to **276**.

255

Your Kai Discipline of Tracking reveals to you that the left tunnel heads north and the right tunnel heads east. Ikaya is about fifty miles to the north.

If you wish to take the left tunnel, turn to **125**.
If you decide to take the right tunnel, turn to **184**.

256

The door crashes shut, sealing the exit to the passage outside. Gradually you become aware of a vibration in the floor; but it lasts for only a few seconds and is followed by a dull *click*. Your gaze is drawn back to the black monolith. A crack has appeared in its surface. It runs the entire circumference of the slab and it is getting wider and wider.

If you wish to prepare for combat, turn to **217**.

If you decide to press yourself into a corner of the chamber, and take cover beneath your cloak, turn to **7**.

257

A shiver runs up your spine as Dyce's screams fade away into the dark gorge. You are staring into the inky blackness when Irian suddenly shouts: 'There . . . over there. I'm sure I saw something.'

You turn to see him pointing not at the gorge but towards the west. 'Look, over there,' says Fenor, who is also pointing, but at a ridge of ice in the middle distance. Two fur-clad warriors are standing on top of a large slab of ice. They stare in your direction alerted no doubt by Dyce's scream.

'Ice Barbarians,' whispers Irian, his voice shaking with fear 'If they reach Ikaya before us, we're as good as dead.'

You are still fifteen miles from the ice fortress and less than three hours of daylight remain.

If you wish to try and outrun the Ice Barbarians, and press on to Ikaya, turn to **327**.

If you decide to attack them to prevent them raising the alarm, turn to **307**.

258

Sweat breaks out on your forehead as you concentrate on shielding your mind from this psychic attack. Your assailant, whoever or whatever it is, is a very powerful enemy; you know that you must rid yourself of the Bracelet if you are to survive the agony of this mind combat. In order to discard the Gold Bracelet, you will have to break your Mindshield.

Pick a number from the *Random Number Table* (0 = 10). If you possess the Kai Discipline of Hunting or Sixth Sense, you may deduct 2 from the number you have picked. The resulting total is the number of ENDURANCE points you lose before ridding yourself of the accursed Bracelet.

If you are still alive, make the necessary adjustments to your *Action Chart* and turn to **63**.

259

Fenor suddenly leaps to his feet and grabs his sword. 'It's a Kalkoth. Quickly, arm yourselves or we are done for.' The others fumble for their weapons as Fenor disappears out into the snow. Almost immediately, there is a piercing scream of agony and something is hurled against the tent. The tent collapses and you find yourself lying face to face with Fenor's mutilated body.

Gripped by sudden fear and panic, you scramble out of the tangled chaos and unsheathe your weapon. The hideous shape of a large, four-legged monster leaps at you. Its red eyes glow like hot coals and its fanged mouth is wide open to reveal a long barbed tongue. It is upon you and you must fight it to the death.

Kalkoth: COMBAT SKILL 11   ENDURANCE 35

If you lose any ENDURANCE points during this combat, turn immediately to **129**.

If you kill the creature without losing any ENDURANCE points, turn to **151**.

260

Due to the surprise of your attack, you strike twice before the Ice Barbarian can react. You do not lose any ENDURANCE points during the first two rounds of combat. If the Ice Barbarian is still alive for the third round of combat, he draws a bone scimitar and attacks you. He is immune to Mindblast.

Ice Barbarian: COMBAT SKILL 17   ENDURANCE 29

If you win the combat, turn to **210**.

261

As you reach the landing below, you stumble and graze your leg. Sprawled on the stone steps, you notice a gap in the left wall. A door has been cunningly concealed by the intricate carvings. Looking more closely, you see a small lever, which you quickly pull.

Turn to **290**.

262

The child kicks and bites at your arm like a wild animal. Pick a number from the *Random Number Table* to see if you manage to hang on to him.

If the number you have picked is *0–6*, turn to **320**.
If the number you have picked is *7–9*, turn to **140**.
If you posses the Kai Discipline of Sixth Sense, turn to **71**.

263

Because the passage is narrow, you must fight the

Kalkoth one at a time. Their long venomous tongues flicker, ready to sting you.

Kalkoth 1: COMBAT SKILL 11   ENDURANCE 35
Kalkoth 2: COMBAT SKILL 10   ENDURANCE 32
Kalkoth 3: COMBAT SKILL 8   ENDURANCE 30

You can evade the fight at any time by turning to **277**.

If you lose any ENDURANCE points during the combat, turn immediately to **66**.

If you win the combat without losing any ENDURANCE points, turn to **25**.

264

You enter a massive chamber, ill-lit and icy cold: a hidden temple of the Ancients. The floor is made from slabs of quartz and granite and is littered with rock and ice. Your eye follows a line of tall pillars leading towards a sacrificial altar set into an alcove in the northern wall. Upon this altar lies a strange statue, which seems to be carved from smooth white stone. At its head and feet, black staves rest upright in holes bored into the altar stone.

To the left of the altar there is a darkened archway, through which a flight of stairs ascends out of view.

If you wish to cross the temple and advance towards the staircase, turn to **60**.

If you wish to cross the temple floor by stepping only on the quartz flagstones, turn to **168**.

If you wish to cross the temple by stepping only on the granite flagstones, turn to **244**.

265 – *Illustration XV*

This strange creature is a Crystal Frostwyrm, a scavenging beast now living on the remains of the unfortunate creatures who have entered the cavern. Its hard skin is almost transparent, and its internal organs can be seen pulsating inside. A large mouth opens in the crystalline head to reveal row upon row of jagged crystal teeth. Your back is pressed to the stone door and there is no way to evade the monster. You must fight the creature to the death. It is immune to Mindblast.

Crystal Frostwyrm: COMBAT SKILL 15 ENDURANCE 30

If you win the combat, turn to **3**.

266

You desperately try to release your foot but the sledge is already toppling into the void. With one last effort, you wrench your foot clear, but it is too late to avoid the fall. As you tumble into the crevasse, you hear the horrified screams of your guides fading above you.

Turn to **21**.

267

Loi-Kymar suddenly points to the pocket in which you have put the Glowing Crystal. 'Why do you carry a Doomstone, Kai Lord? Are you unaware of the danger it holds?'

You quickly remove the Crystal and show it to the magician. 'Agh!' he cries, as if to look upon it causes him pain. 'Cast it away before we both succumb to

XV.   This strange creature is a Crystal Frostwyrm and you must
fight it to the death

the sickness. It is a cursed gem of the Ancients, it can only bring sickness and death to any mortal who covets its beauty.' Reluctantly, you obey Loi-Kymar's wishes and throw the Crystal away. Make the necessary adjustment to your *Action Chart*.

Turn to **44**.

268

You manage to crack the seal in exactly the right place, and thereby avoid smashing the thin glass stem. The vapour rising from the black liquid is sharp and pungent.

If you have ever visited the Graveyard of the Ancients, turn to **177**.

If you have not, you quickly replace the stopper of the Vial. The vapour is making you nauseous, and you decide against keeping this suspicious fluid. Return to **10** and choose your next course of action.

269

You reach a tunnel on the far side of the chasm and follow it for many miles. You eventually arrive at an enormous chamber, the ceiling of which towers five hundred feet above you. An icy wind, blowing through the many fissures that crack the ceiling, whips around the hall.

If you wish to search for a way of climbing up and out through the fissures, turn to **335**.

If you decide to press on and look for an exit on the far side of the hall, turn to **182**.

270

The Ice Barbarians are taken completely by surprise. You have killed one of them before the other has time to react to your attack. He is unarmed but determined to fight you.

Ice Barbarian: COMBAT SKILL 14   ENDURANCE 25

If you win the combat, turn to **340**.

271

Your attack has caused the Ice Barbarian scout to lose his balance. He tumbles in a flurry of snow and broken skis. The fur-clad child rolls clear of his father's backpack and lies face downwards in the snow, less than ten feet away.

The Ice Barbarian scout is badly dazed by the fall, but is already attempting to stagger to his feet.

If you wish to attack the Ice Barbarian scout before he fully regains his senses, turn to **241**.

If you wish to grab the child as a hostage and try to escape, turn to **262**.

272

As the vile Akraa'Neonor quivers and dies, Vonotar breaks off mind combat and runs back towards the Brumalmarc throne.

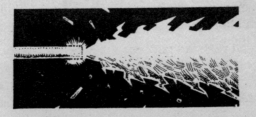

Loi-Kymar is badly shaken but he has survived the ordeal. He quickly joins you at the edge of the moat and casts a handful of herbs down into the darkness. Within seconds, a mass of vines and creepers coil upwards to form a bridge. You are halfway across the bridge when Vonotar suddenly reappears, a crystal rod held high in his hand. He takes aim at the mass of creepers and a chilling cone of frost hurtles from its tip.

If you possess the Sommerswerd, turn to **213**.

If you do not possess it, pick a number from the *Random Number Table*.

If the number you have picked is *0–3*, turn to **143**.

If the number you have picked is *4–9*, turn to **58**.

273

You are to travel to Ikaya by sledge. Two sledges have been loaded with enough food, and equipment for the mission, each drawn by a team of six Kanu-dogs. This sturdy breed are native to Kalte and make ideal sledge dogs. Their thick tawny coats and powerful chests, as well as their renowned vigour and enthusiasm make them well-suited to the harsh work ahead.

Your three guides, Irian, Fenor and Dyce, are all experienced trappers. They are skilled at survival in this icy desert, and have experienced its many unseen dangers. Once the dogs are in harness, you and Irian climb aboard your sledge and signal to the others to lead the way.

Staring across the frozen expanse of the Ljuk ice shelf, you see the white glare of the Hrod Basin edge. '"Ice-blink" they call it,' says Irian, his eyes glinting from deep inside the hood of his fur jacket. 'It's the reflection of the ice shelf. It looks no more than four miles away at most, but it's nearer forty than four. The air of Kalte can be very deceptive.'

The weather is bright and windless and you make excellent progress on the first day. As darkness sets in, you decide to set up camp for the night. The sledges are drawn together, and the tent is erected in the salient away from the wind.

> If you have the Kai Discipline of Sixth Sense, turn to **35**.
> If you do not possess this skill, turn to **112**.

274

You carefully examine the altar, and the two black staves protruding from its surface. The crackling arc of energy that linked these staves seemed to die at the very moment you plunged the Sommerswerd into the cyclonic demon. You notice that where the statue had lain, two stone buttons have now risen from the surface of the altar.

> If you have the Kai Discipline of Sixth Sense, turn to **131**.
> If you wish to press the buttons, turn to **227**.
> If you wish to leave the temple, turn to **306**.

275

The tunnel is low and narrow and gradually descends towards the light of a distant cavern. As you reach the tunnel's end, you peer cautiously into the cavern beyond, in case you disturb something better left alone. Your caution is well placed, for in the centre of the icy cavern lie two large furry creatures. The remains of a shredded carcass lie on the snow around them.

If you have the Kai Discipline of Hunting, Tracking or Animal Kinship, turn to **293**.

If you do not possess any of the above skills, turn to **197**.

276

You soon reach the junction where the corridor meets another running from east to west.

If you wish to head east, turn to **349**.

If you decide to go west, turn to **50**.

If you have the Kai Discipline of Hunting or Tracking, turn to **219**.

277

You run back into the cave as fast as you can, but the Kalkoth are familiar with this route and they are gaining on you. As you reach the frozen waterfall, you notice the slab of a silvery mineral overhanging the cave mouth.

If you possess a weapon, you may strike this outcrop and attempt to block the cave, by turning to **142**.

If you do not, you will have to stand and fight the creatures as they emerge from the cave. Turn to **32**.

278

Your first blow scatters the bones of the skeleton all over the chamber. It seems that it was nothing more than the harmless remains of an old tomb guard. A closer examination of the sword reveals that the blackness is nothing more than pitted iron. You lower your weapon and slowly climb the stairs.

Turn to **36**.

279

Baknar are known to sleep for up to three days after a feast. By the number of freshly stripped bones littering the chamber, this Baknar is likely to be asleep for many hours. You slip past the snoring creature and leave the chamber.

Turn to **235**.

280

The Key is coated with a corrosive digestive acid that burns through your mittens and attacks your fingers. Lose 1 ENDURANCE point. You drop the Key and plunge your hand into the snow to ease the pain. If you still wish to keep the key, you can wipe it in the snow before placing it in your pocket, but remember to mark it on your *Action Chart* as a Special Item. You must now search for a way of opening the fortress door.

Turn to **344**.

281

You cover your nose with your sleeve and turn away from the carcass. Irian has regained consciousness, and is quick to begin scooping out some Baknar oil for himself.

The light is fading fast and you decide to pitch camp here for the night. After a meal has been prepared and eaten, you volunteer to sit watch, in case the Baknar should decide to return. Spending a sleepless night huddled against the cold night winds seems infinitely preferable to sharing a tent with your guides stinking of Baknar oil.

Turn to **325**.

282

The Ice Barbarian was armed with a Spear. You may take this Weapon if you wish. You search the body and discover a curious disc of blue stone. If you wish to keep the Blue Stone Disc, put it in your pocket and mark it on your *Action Chart* as a Special Item.

At the top of the stairs, if you wish to go left (north), turn to **104**.
If you wish to go right (south), turn to **330**.

283

The door is closing fast; there is very little space left through which to escape.

Pick a number from the *Random Number Table*. If you have the Kai Discipline of Hunting, you may add 3 to the number you have picked.

If your total is now *0–4*, turn to **53**.
If your total is now *5–7*, turn to **16**.
If your total is now *8–12*, turn to **113**.

284

After a few hundred yards, you find yourself in a huge cavern that spreads out in all directions as far as the eye can see. You have entered the caverns of Kalte and are now looking at an uncharted world that few

Sommlending have ever seen. This massive underground labyrinth was constructed by the Ancients many ages before the Sommlending set foot in Magnamund. Its wide avenues, temples and arenas once echoed to the sounds of a race of creatures for whom the ice was a natural home. M'lare bowls still hang from the ceiling bathing the caverns in their eternal light.

You trek steadily northwards for nearly six hours, until you arrive at the bank of a fast flowing meltwater river. On the opposite bank, you see a tunnel leading off into the distance. You can find no apparent way of crossing the deep water, except by using the ice-floes bobbing up and down on the surface. By jumping from one floe to the next, you could get to the opposite bank, but it will not be easy. You will have to jump at least three of the icy slabs to reach the other side.

Pick a number from the *Random Number Table*. If you have the Kai Discipline of Hunting, you may add 2 to the number you have picked. If your current ENDURANCE points total is less than 8, deduct 2 from the number you have picked.

If your total score is now *−2−+3*, turn to **94**.
If your total score is now *4−11*, turn to **176**.

285

As the door slides back, you are horrified to see the blank pupil-less eyes of the Ice Barbarian staring directly at your face. A low, unnatural cry comes from his open mouth, and in an instant the Doomwolves are awake and snarling.

(contd over)

If you wish to escape, you must turn and run back down the stairs. Turn to **261**.

If you wish to stand and fight, turn to **343**.

286

The lance has grazed your shoulder blade and knocked you to the ground. As you scramble to your feet, you see that the Ice Barbarian scout has stopped and removed his skis. He advances towards you with an evil-looking bone sword in his hand. You prepare for combat.

Turn to **68**.

287

The Ice Barbarian screams a low, unnatural cry. You have been spotted and you know you must silence him quickly before he alerts the whole of Ikaya to your presence. You turn to fight.

Turn to **161**.

288

That night, a gale sweeps across the open ice shelf and buries your tent in snow. During your sleep, the canvas is forced in upon the four of you and your sleeping furs become soaking wet. You awake at dawn with terrible cramp in both of your legs. It takes nearly an hour of massaging your frozen limbs before you can stand properly. You are beginning to wish that you had never set foot in this icy hell.

Turn to **167**.

289

You manage to remove most of the hardened wax that covers the stopper, and ease the reluctant seal from the fragile glass stem.

If you have the Kai Discipline of Animal Kinship or if you have reached the Kai rank of Aspirant (you are skilled in six Kai Disciplines) or above, turn to **156**.

If you do not possess this Kai Discipline, or if you have not yet reached the required Kai rank, you are suspicious of the dank mouldy smell of this liquid. You quickly put the Vial down. Now return to **10** and choose your next course of action.

290

The stone door moves slowly to one side. It reveals a narrow archway that is full of billowing and swirling mist, hiding whatever it is that lurks beyond. You notice a severe drop in temperature.

If you have the Kai Discipline of Sixth Sense and if you have reached the Kai rank of Guardian (you are skilled in seven Kai Disciplines), turn to **341**.

If you have the Kai Discipline of Sixth Sense but have not yet reached the rank of Guardian, turn to **124**.

If you do not have the Kai Discipline of Sixth Sense, you prepare yourself to fight and pass through the misty arch. Turn to **264**.

291

When you awake, you sense that something has changed. It takes nearly a minute to realize that the incessant howling of the night winds has ceased. 'It's a beautiful morning,' says Irian cheerfully, his head appearing through the tent flap. You quickly climb out of your sleeping furs and stare out over the icy landscape. The Kalte air is fresh and clear. You see a strong mirage in the distance that seems to throw the land up much higher than it could possibly be.

'We should make it to "The Rock" by nightfall,' says Fenor, as he busily pulls a reluctant Kanu-dog into its harness. 'Best to make camp there tonight. The shelter is good; this far from the sea, a blizzard can whip across the shelf from nowhere in a few minutes. I've known trappers to be blown for miles if they're careless or unlucky enough to be caught out on the shelf with no cover.'

That day, the Kanu-dogs pull strong and true, for the going is smooth across the ice shelf. By nightfall, you have reached 'The Rock', a splinter of granite that has thrust through the ice shelf. Its curious shape reminds you of the King's citadel in Holmgard. You make camp to the leeward side of 'The Rock', to avoid the worst of the night winds.

Pick a number from the *Random Number Table*.

If the number you have picked is *0–4*, turn to **103**.
If the number you have picked is *5–9*, turn to **220**.

292 – *Illustration XVI (overleaf)*

The massive door slides open to reveal a long stone causeway, spanning a vast chamber that is bathed in the orange glow of fiery furnaces. A gust of hot, putrid air wafts over you and a deafening noise assails your ears. Fifty feet below the causeway, great stone vats hang suspended over roaring flames. Each vat is full of bubbling slime writhing and contorting as if it were alive.

Fear and revulsion grip your stomach as you begin to grasp the sinister secret of this hall. Row upon row of stone plinths bear the mutilated corpses of Ice Barbarians, their skins peeled back and pinned open. Each corpse is attended by hideous creatures, a ghoulish legion of mutants crawling and slithering across the blood-drenched floor. This hall is a place of great evil, a nightmarish laboratory, a temple of the Black Art of Necromancy constructed by Vonotar the Traitor.

Across the causeway, another doorway suddenly slides back to reveal four Ice Barbarian mutants. As they shuffle towards you, a mixture of horror and pity overwhelms your senses.

If you wish to fight these creatures, turn to **83**.
If you wish to flee from this terrible place, turn to **130**.

XVI.   This hall is a place of great evil, a nightmare laboratory

293

The creatures in this cavern are Kalkoth, savage and cruel predators of Kalte. Their favourite prey is Baknar, and it is the remains of one of those animals spattered across the floor of the cavern. There is another passage leading off towards the north, but it is on the far side of the cavern.

If you wish to creep past the sleeping Kalkoth, turn to **125**.

If you wish to retrace your steps and take the other tunnel heading north, turn to **235**.

If you wish to attack these sleeping creatures, turn to **109**.

294

Destroying the door in this way is an extremely strenuous task. You will need to eat two Meals after the six hours of labour or lose 6 ENDURANCE points due to fatigue.

When you finally cut a hole large enough through which to escape, you discover that you have attracted some unwanted attention.

Turn to **106**.

295

On seeing you enter, the two old men jump to their feet and flee from the chamber along a smaller passageway. Their screams of panic echo loudly throughout the caverns.

You are very hungry and quickly consume the cooked animal, pausing only to spit out the bones. You then notice that the fire is burning in a strange, half-spherical metal bowl. The other half of the sphere lies on the icy floor nearby and you find that both halves fit together perfectly. When you open it, you discover that the fire still burns inside. If you wish to keep this Firesphere, place it inside your jacket and mark it on your *Action Chart* as a Special Item.

Return to the tunnel by turning to **132**.

296

Unfortunately, the guards suspect that something is amiss and challenge you in their strange language. You have no alternative but to attack them before they can raise the alarm. However, the fumes of the smoking herbs are affecting the Ice Barbarians and this will aid you in the following combat. You need fight only 3 rounds of combat before the guards collapse unconscious to the floor.

Ice Barbarians: COMBAT SKILL 17   ENDURANCE 30

If you are still alive after the combat, you can signal to Loi-Kymar to approach the hall.

To your delight you discover that one of the magnificent jewelled doors is unlocked. You gently push it ajar and enter Vonotar's chamber.

Turn to **173**.

297

You have been walking along the passage for less than five minutes when it veers sharply northwards. Just ahead, to your left you can see a large stone door; the lever is up and the door is closed.

If you wish to pull the lever and open the door, turn to **317**.

If you wish to continue northwards, turn to **126**.

298

You discover a curious Triangle of Blue Stone attached to a chain. It is held tightly in the skeletal hand of one of the corpses, and you are forced to smash the fingerbones in order to examine the necklace more closely. If you wish to keep this Blue Stone Triangle, slip it over your head and wear it inside your jacket. Mark it on your *Action Chart* as a Special Item.

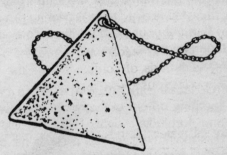

You may leave the chamber by a tunnel in the far wall, by turning to **315**.

Or you can retrace your route and take the other tunnel by turning to **125**.

299

Unless you have used the Kai Discipline of Mind Over Matter, bolts of blue energy leap from the black staves and catch you squarely in the chest. You are thrown backwards by the force of the charge, and left lying on the cold temple floor. You lose 2 ENDURANCE points. If you used the Kai Discipline of Mind Over

300

Matter, the raw energy arcs harmlessly between the two staves and you are not injured.

If you wish to try to activate the buttons again, turn to **65**.

If you wish to leave the temple, turn to **306**.

300

For three days and nights, you trek northwards across the bleak and inhospitable glacier. Irian and Fenor have both suffered from severe snow-blindness, and the relentless north wind seems to sap everyone's strength. On the morning of the fourth day on the glacier, the wind finally drops. A bearing can now be taken to find out your exact position. To everyone's dismay Irian announces that you have veered a long way off course.

You turn to face the ancient grey peaks of a mountain range, looming up out of the northern snow. It is a bleak and forbidding sight. 'The Myjaviks,' says Dyce, disappointment written all over his bearded face. 'We've come too far east.'

The Myjavik Mountains now lie between you and Ikaya. To cross them will mean having to leave the sledges and Kanu-dogs, packing your equipment on your backs and continuing on foot. There is an alternative, but it could lose you two precious days: you can retrace your route to the glacier and resume the march from there.

If you wish to abandon the dogs and sledges, and cross the Myjavik Mountains on foot, turn to **12**.

If you decide to lose two days and trace your way back to the Viad Glacier, turn to **238**.

301

'We're on the same level as the Hall of the Brumalmarc,' whispers Loi-Kymar, peering through a crack in the kitchen door. 'It's at the end of this corridor.'

Two Ice Barbarians stand beside the jewel-encrusted doors that lead to the great hall. They are covered from head to toe in strange bone armour, and armed with crystal swords. The old wizard steps back from the door and says: 'We must deal with them silently and swiftly.' He takes three jars from his pockets and mutters a strange incantation as he mixes the contents together in a stone bowl. There is a pitcher of water on the table. He splashes a few drops on to the herbs, and wisps of blue smoke arise. 'This will silence the guards if we can move it close enough to them.'

> If you have the Kai Discipline of Camouflage, turn to **122**.
> If you have the Kai Discipline of Mind Over Matter, turn to **228**.
> If you have the Kai Discipline of Hunting, turn to **347**.
> If you do not possess any of the above Kai Disciplines, turn to **179**.

302

You have descended over two hundred feet before you finally reach the bottom of the crevasse. It is completely dark except for a pinpoint of light in the far distance. You head towards the light, but progress is slow and painful. Large chunks of broken rock and ice litter the crevasse floor, and in the darkness you are constantly walking into, or falling over them.

Pick a number from the *Random Number Table*. If you have the Kai Discipline of Sixth Sense, you may add 2 to the number you have picked.

If your total is now *0–1*, turn to **37**.
If your total is now *2–7*, turn to **193**.
If your total is now *8–11*, turn to **243**.

303

You insert the Key and turn it clockwise. A click confirms that it works. Slowly the shank of the Key slips from your grip and disappears into the lock and the great stone lid opens to reveal a magnificent Silver Helmet.

If you wish to put this splendid Helmet on your head, turn to **308**.
If you decide to leave the Helmet where it is, you can explore the stairs by turning to **323**.

304

The mighty sword illuminates the passage with its golden glow. The Helghast shrieks a hideous cry and retreats, its eyes glowing a fiery red with hatred and fear. It recognizes the power you wield, a force that spells death and eternal destruction to its kind. In blind panic, it attacks you with a powerful Mindblast. Unless you possess the Kai Discipline of Mindshield, you must lose 2 ENDURANCE points for every round of combat you fight with this creature. It is immune to Mindblast. However, because the creature is one of the undead, remember to double all ENDURANCE points that it loses due to the power of the Sommerswerd.

Helghast: COMBAT SKILL 22   ENDURANCE 30

If you win the combat, turn to **20**.

305 – *Illustration XVII (overleaf)*

The heavy beast rolls off the sledge and lies motionless on the ice. Fenor has managed to light a torch and is thrusting the flaming brand at the other two Baknar. They are terrified by the fire and quickly turn and flee. You cheer as they disappear and turn to congratulate your brave guides, but are stunned to see that they have already started to skin the dead Baknar. You watch with disgust as Dyce opens the beast from throat to belly with his sharp hunting knife. He quickly pulls back the white fur and scoops out handfuls of thick oil from under the skin. The smell of this oil is horrible, so horrible in fact that even the Kanu-dogs bury their noses into the snow to avoid it. You cannot believe your eyes when the two guides start to rub this vile oil all over their faces and inside their clothes.

'Baknar oil,' shouts Fenor enthusiastically. 'Nothing

XVII.   They have already started to skin the dead Baknar

like it for keeping warm and dry.' He pulls his hand from the dead beast and offers you a fistful of the putrid jelly.

If you wish to accept his offer, turn to **8**.
If the thought of smelling like a vat of rancid cheese does not appeal to you, turn to **281**.

306

As you pass through the archway, you notice a lever set into the dark stone wall. You pull it and a door slides across, sealing the temple behind you. The temperature is warmer and you can hear a low rumbling sound somewhere in the distance. Ahead, you can see a light at the end of a dark passageway. You discover that it is shining out of an oblong portal, close to the floor, through which you can see a corridor ten feet below.

If you wish to squeeze through the portal and drop into the corridor, turn to **206**.
If you decide to continue along the passage, turn to **6**.

307

Preparing yourself for combat, you signal to the others to attack. The Ice Barbarians soon realize the danger and flee towards the west. To your dismay, you see that they are equipped with skis and can make a speedy escape. They have small poles attached to their fur-clad backs from which strange blue flags flutter. 'Convoy scouts,' says Irian, shielding his eyes from the glare of the snow. 'Their blue "Banach" – their backflags – mean they're scouts from a sledge pack. They're probably on their way back from the trading post at Ljuk; their convoy can't be more than a few miles away – five at the most.'

If you wish to press on to Ikaya and try to outrun the Ice Barbarians before they return with reinforcements, turn to **327**.

If you wish to follow the scouts westwards and find out more about their convoy, turn to **178**.

308

Despite its size, the Helmet feels light and comfortable. Mark it on your *Action Chart* as a Special Item. If worn during combat, it will increase your COMBAT SKILL by 2 points. The lid of the chest slowly closes and you leave the chamber, elated by your magnificent discovery. You continue along the corridor and explore the staircase ahead.

Turn to **323**.

309

You make a quick search of the bodies and discover that one of them has a triangle of blue stone hanging by a chain around his neck. If you wish to keep this Item, put the chain round your neck and mark it as a Special Item on your *Action Chart*.

You are very hungry and you quickly consume the cooked animal, pausing only to spit out its bones. Then you notice that the fire is burning in a strange, half-spherical metal bowl. The other half of the sphere lies on the icy floor nearby. You find that both halves fit together perfectly. When you open them, you discover that the fire still burns inside.

If you wish to keep this Firesphere, put it inside your jacket and mark it on your *Action Chart* as a Special Item.

You finish the last scraps of food, and return to the tunnel.

Turn to **132**.

310

You break open the Firesphere and an intense howl fills your ears. The cyclone halts. It will not advance towards you whilst you hold this sphere of guttering flame.

If you wish to leave the temple, turn to **306**.
If you wish to search the altar and alcove, turn to **72**.

311

You recognize the Potion to be distilled Alether, a potion of strength. Your Kai masters used Alether to increase their COMBAT SKILL in battle, and there is enough concentrated Alether in this Vial to increase your COMBAT SKILL by 4 for the duration of one combat. For it to be effective you must swallow it immediately before you fight. If you wish to keep this Vial, mark it on your *Action Chart* as a Backpack Item.

Now return to **10** and choose your next course of action.

312

You desperately claw at your foot, but the sledge is already beginning to fall into the crevasse. As you tumble hundreds of feet into the void, the last sound that you hear are the horrified cries of your guides fading above you.

Your life and your mission end here.

313

The mutants lie dead at your feet. You are about to step over them and attack their controller, when more of the unfortunate wretches appear at his side. You are greatly outnumbered and you must escape now, or you will surely perish in this evil hall. You sprint back to the door and run the length of the main corridor, as fast as your shaking legs will carry you.

Turn to **130**.

314

You have explored only a hundred yards of the rockface when you discover a large fissure – the entrance to a cave. In your eagerness to escape from the bitter wind you quickly enter and, in the darkness, fail to notice the crevasse that divides this cave in two. In a tumble of ice and stone, you fall head first into the dark.

Turn to **240**.

315

You soon reach a large hall where the pressure of the moving ice has opened a large crevasse in the floor. The crevasse is over sixty feet wide, and there is no apparent way of crossing it. As you stare into the chasm, you notice that rough steps have been cut into the side, descending into the darkness.

If you wish to descend these steps, turn to **302**.
If you decide to retrace your route to the other tunnel entrance, turn to **125**.

316

There is an aura of power encircling the Gold Bracelet that makes you feel uneasy. The Ice Barbarians rely on tooth and bone for their weapons because there are no mines in Kalte. Not only gold but all metals are considered rare and precious; you have never heard of the Ice Barbarians trading their furs for any metal other than steel. Jewellery is of no interest to these hard and cruel hunters. You suspect that this Bracelet was worn by force and not by choice. If you wish to take and wear the Gold Bracelet, mark it on your *Action Chart* as a Special Item.

If you take the Bracelet, turn to **236**.
If you decide to leave it, make your way along the corridor towards the distant junction by turning to **215**.

317

The stone portal creaks open but grinds to an abrupt halt halfway across. The gap is a little over two feet wide and you are only just able to squeeze through to the chamber beyond. The air in the room is cold and stale; this chamber has obviously lain undisturbed for many thousands of years. Stone shelves are stacked high with bottles and flasks. On a table in the centre lies a beautiful pack full of different coloured potions.

If you wish to examine these ancient potions, turn to **10**.

If you wish to leave the chamber and continue northwards, turn to **126**.

318

You can sense that the Baknar is desperate for food. Your Kai Discipline will be useless, for you will not be able to order it away from the camp now that it has detected the Kanu-dogs. However, you know that Baknar are fearless hunters, fearless except when it comes to one thing – fire. Grabbing a torch from a pile of equipment, you light it and race out of the tent. It is dark and snowing heavily, but a movement to your right betrays the Baknar as it lopes towards you. It is preparing to pounce when the sight of the guttering flames makes it shriek with terror. A second later, it has turned and disappeared into the night.

The Kanu-dogs are safe, but to make sure that the Baknar does not return, you agree to take it in turns to sit watch with a torch and a weapon.

Turn to **134**.

319

You take careful aim and throw the Gold Crowns along the corridor. Distracted by the sudden noise, the warrior draws his bone sword and investigates. Your plan has worked; he is busy searching for Gold Crowns on his hands and knees and he fails to see you creep past and ascend the stairs. Remember to adjust the number of Gold Crowns on your *Action Chart*.

Turn to **332**.

320 – *Illustration XVIII (overleaf)*

You manage to hang on to the struggling child, and remove a bone dagger from his boot to prevent him stabbing you in the back.

The Ice Barbarians have drawn themselves up into a circle around you, but they dare not attack while you are holding one of their children as a hostage. Holding the bone dagger to the child's throat, you slowly inch your way towards the sledge. You soon realize that you will never be able to outdistance them on a loaded sledge. You will have to think of something – and quickly.

If you wish to cut the equipment loose, free the Ice Barbarian child, and escape on the unloaded sledge, turn to **190**.

(contd over)

XVIII.   The Ice Barbarians circle around you but they dare not attack while you hold one of their children as hostage

If you wish to cut loose the equipment but keep the
    boy with you as a hostage during your escape,
    turn to **33**.

321

You follow the twisting ice passage for many miles
until you stumble upon a grotto. A small melt-water
stream divides the cavern and another passage leads
off towards the north. As you jump across the narrow
stream, you notice a small Blue Triangle of Stone
lying in the icy water attached to a neck chain. If you
wish to keep the Blue Stone Triangle, put it around
your neck and tuck it into your jacket. Mark it on your
Action Chart as a Special Item.

A brighter light emanates from the passage ahead,
and you can see a large hall in the distance.

Turn to **235**.

322

As you race across the slippery surface, the ice begins
to crack. Glancing behind, you see the Kalkoth has
stopped at the edge of the lake. It seems to be terrified
of the dark shadow that you saw earlier under the ice;
the shadow that has just reappeared less than twenty
feet from where you are now. With panic rising in
your throat, you turn and run, praying all the way for
the ice and your luck to hold out.

Pick a number from the *Random Number Table*.

If the number you have picked is *0–2*, turn to **153**.
If the number you have picked is *3–9*, turn to **59**.

323

You climb over a hundred stone steps before arriving
at a narrow landing.

(contd over)

Pick a number from the *Random Number Table*. If you have the Kai Discipline of Sixth Sense, Tracking or Hunting, add 3 to this number.

> If your total is now *0–4*, turn to **76**.
> If your total is now *5–12*, turn to **2**.

324

As the vile Akraa'Neonor dies at your feet, you glimpse the hunchback descending from his platform and scurrying off towards a distant door. You turn to chase him but freeze when you see the body of Loi-Kymar lying motionless below. He is dead, killed in psychic combat with the traitor. With anger welling up inside, you raise your weapon and sprint after Vonotar, now intent upon his death.

The door leads to a long corridor, at the end of which is a curtained arch. You tear the curtain aside and continue on your chase.

Turn to **61**.

325

The next morning arrives bright and windless. The sun pierces the thin layer of cloud, bathing the east in a soft pink glow. This beautiful vision reminds you that your Kai masters once told you that the light of Kalte is unlike anywhere else in Magnamund. With tent and equipment packed, you leave the pass and venture out on to the Hrod Basin; one hundred miles of open ice now lie between you and Storm Giant Pass.

At first, the journey is easy. The Basin has been worn smooth by the wind and no crevasses lurk unseen beneath the hard, dense snow. But at dawn on the third day, events take a turn for the worse. You are awoken from a deep sleep by Dyce shaking your shoulder. He is frightened. 'What's wrong?' you ask, still bleary-eyed and sleepy.

'Ice Barbarians . . . on the horizon. Twenty, maybe more. Five wind sledges and a warrior escort. I think they've seen us.'

In an instant, you have all climbed out of your sleeping furs and begun to pack away the tent. Dyce is correct, they are Ice Barbarians and they are heading towards you from the west. 'If they catch us, we're as good as dead,' says Fenor, as he ties the last of the equipment to the sledge.

The Ice Barbarians of Kalte are a fierce and warlike race of nomads. For thousands of years they have travelled this icy wasteland, trapping furs and herding mammoths. Their only contact with the rest of Magnamund is through the trading post of Ljuk. In summer, when the coast around Ljuk is free from ice, they journey there to trade their furs for weapons and tools, as there is no iron or wood in Kalte. They hate all except their own kind, and kill anyone they find who dares to trespass in their icy domain. You soon hear their war-cries less than three miles distant, and for the first time since you landed, you pray for a blizzard to hide your escape.

Turn to **216**.

326

After a period of intense concentration, the image of the lock gradually takes form in your mind. The lock is shielded by a spell, but your Kai skill and your determination prove the stronger power. A *click* confirms the success of your effort, but you are greatly fatigued and lose 1 ENDURANCE point. Then silently, and of its own accord, the great stone lid opens to reveal a magnificent Silver Helmet.

If you wish to put this Helmet on, turn to **308**.

If you would rather leave it where it is, you can explore the stairs by turning to **323**.

If you have the Kai Discipline of Sixth Sense, turn to **127**.

327

As you approach nearer to Ikaya, the recent encounter with the Ice Barbarians plays on your mind. Will you be able to outrun them or are they planning an ambush at this very moment? Both Irian and Fenor look very anxious and little is said as you trek across the difficult terrain. But your worries distract your attention from more familiar danger. You are less than eight miles from the fortress when the snow gives way beneath you and you plunge into a hidden crevasse.

Pick a number from the *Random Number Table*.

If the number you have picked is *0–8*, turn to **105**.

If the number you have picked is *9*, turn to **144**.

328

In spite of his frail physique, the man climbs with surprising speed and dexterity. You pull him through the portal and retrieve your Rope. 'The stairs,' he says, pointing into the darkness. 'Our escape lies that way, but you had best take the lead; my eyes ail me. I have suffered the snow-blindness and my vision is just a blur.'

You pack your Rope and lead the way along the passage. You are about to descend the stairs when a pair of skeletal hands close around your throat from behind. A hideous cry betrays the 'merchant's' true identity. He is a Helghast, a deadly shape-changing servant of the Darklords, and he has tricked you into releasing him from his cell. He is intent on murdering you.

You desperately gasp for air as the skeletal fingers tear and burn at your throat. You lose 6 ENDURANCE points. If you are still alive, you can break free from his steely grip. You must now fight this creature to the death. Due to the surprise of the Helghast's attack and the injury it has inflicted on your throat, you are unable to swallow any potions prior to the combat.

If you possess the Sommerswerd, turn to **99**.
If you do not possess it, turn to **175**.

329

The noises that you hear are Kalkoth. There are three of these vicious creatures, inhabitants of the mountains of Kalte. They are predatory killers and their favourite prey is Baknar.

If you have smeared Baknar oil into your skin, turn to **202**.

If you have not applied Baknar oil to your skin, you can avoid the Kalkoth by retracing your route back to the entrance of the other tunnel, by turning to **284**.

(contd over)

If you wish to attack the creatures, you can turn to **138**.

You soon arrive at the bottom of a spiral staircase; there seems to be no alternative but to climb it. After ascending over two hundred steps, you arrive at a long passage which ends at a balcony. Thirty feet below, you see Vonotar the Traitor standing in front of two Ice Barbarian warriors. He is placing a gold bracelet upon the wrist of one of them, and is unaware of your presence. There are no stairs from here to the chamber below, but there is a door at the end of the balcony.

If you have a Rope, you can climb down and attempt to capture him by turning to **100**.

If you do not have a Rope, you can descend the spiral staircase by turning to **148**.

If you prefer, you can investigate the door at the end of the balcony by turning to **61**.

331

The following day, the weather becomes bitterly cold. Wind from the north brings a hail of ice that stings your face. Your lips soon split and bleed. By midday, you are engulfed in a blizzard that makes progress slow and tiring. The howling wind forces you to dismount from your sledge and push it. You feel utterly exhausted. Your hands and toes are numb with the cold; the sweat from your exertions freezes to your skin, lining your boots and mittens with a layer of ice.

By the time you reach the glacier's edge, it is nearly nightfall. You are all so exhausted that you barely have the energy to pitch your tent and eat a Meal. Disaster has all but overtaken you. You have frostbite in your toes, fingers and nose, and unless you have the Kai Discipline of Healing, you lose 4 ENDURANCE points.

Pick a number from the *Random Number Table*.

If the number you have picked is *0–4*, turn to **62**.
If the number you have picked is *5–9*, turn to **288**.

332

At the top of the stairs is a wide landing where a corridor runs north to south.

If you wish to head north, turn to **104**.
If you wish to go south, turn to **69**.
If you have the Kai Discipline of Sixth Sense or Hunting, turn to **249**.

333

Your lightning reactions have saved you. The tip of the Ice Barbarian's lance tears your sleeve, but that is all. But, in an instant, the scout has turned and halted He unfastens his skis with one swift, practised action, and draws a bone sword. You must prepare for combat.

Turn to **68**.

334 – *Illustration XIX*

A hidden panel opens near the right stave. Inside, you discover a beautiful Glowing Crystal. It is warm to the touch. If you wish to keep this Glowing Crystal, slip it into your pocket and mark it on your *Action Chart* as a Special Item.

If you wish to activate the buttons again, turn to **65**.
If you wish to leave the temple, turn to **306**.

335

You find that the icy rockface offers many hand-holds, but you cannot find a secure grip with your fur mittens on; but if you remove your mittens in order to climb, you know that frostbite is inevitable.

If you wish to risk your life and your hands, you can continue to climb by turning to **55**.
If you decide to abandon your climb, you can descend to the hall below and search for another exit by turning to **182**.

336

You have covered less than twenty yards when you arrive at the foot of another staircase. You ascend to the top where you see a faint light in the distance, spreading along the floor of the dirt encrusted passage. It is another portal. Through the opening, you can see an old man huddled in the corner of a cell

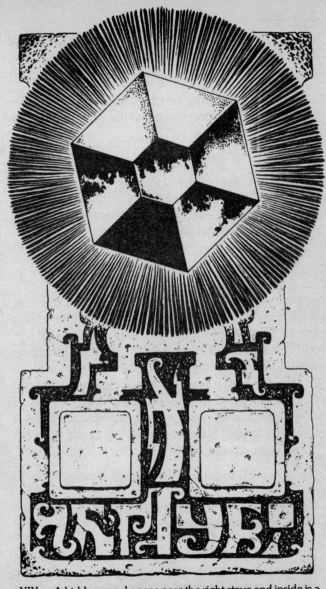

XIX.   A hidden panel opens near the right stave and inside is a
beautiful glowing crystal

twenty feet below. His hair is matted and the dirt that clings to his blue robes almost obscures the crescents and stars embroidered on them.

If you wish to call to the old man, turn to **247**.
If you wish to continue along the passage, turn to **30**.

337

The scout flashes past and stops less than twenty feet away. With a well-practised action, he removes his skis in an instant and draws a vicious looking bone sword. You must prepare for combat.

Turn to **68**.

338

As you step over the bodies of the Ice Barbarians, you catch a glimpse of a grotesque creature staring at you from the corner of a passage to your left. Even though you see it for the briefest moment, it is long enough to send a shiver down your spine. It resembles an enormous man's head. But one that has sprouted feet and a long scaly tail. Although it wears a hooded cloak, there is no trace of a torso beneath it. As it scurries off, your heart pounds at the thought of what horrors may lie ahead.

If you wish to pursue the strange creature, turn to **87**.
If you wish to search the bodies of the dead Ice Barbarians, turn to **26**.

339

Within ten minutes, frostbite has eaten into your hands and feet. On this exposed rockface the icy winds often exceed a speed of one hundred miles an hour. You last for thirty minutes before severe exposure robs you of all consciousness, and you plummet to your death three thousand feet below.

Your mission and your life end here.

340

You drag the bodies out of the kitchen and prop them behind the secret door. When you return, Loi-Kymar is busy examining the bottles of herbs that line the kitchen shelves. He pockets several jars and mixes the contents of two others in a small stone bowl. He offers you a handful of the dry leaves and urges you to eat them. 'They will restore your strength, Lone Wolf.' You eat the sweet tasting herbs and feel a warm glow radiating throughout your body. Restore 6 ENDURANCE points to your current total.

Turn to **301**.

341

You can sense the presence of a powerful life-force beyond the misty arch. As you concentrate, you suddenly recall a tale told to you when you were a small child, 'The Legend of the Vagadyn Gate'. This was a tale of Ice Demons and how they once fought a war to be able to leave their world and come to Kalte. They were formless creatures, without shape and substance, and existed as pure energy in another dimension, beyond the confines of space and time. The Ice Demons discovered the Vagadyn gate, a sort of door between their world and Magnamund; they fought each other to enter this gate, unaware of the fate that awaited them. The Ancients had also discovered the gate. As the Ice Demons passed through the Vagadyn, their spirits were imprisoned in crystals by the cunning Ancients, who harnessed the power of the Ice Demons to build Ikaya. The M'lare bowls that light the fortress each contain the spirits of lesser Ice Demons trapped within. You also remember that the tale warns against destroying the crystal prisons: if an Ice Demon is released it will seek to claim the body of its rescuer.

Forewarned by your Kai skill, you enter the misty arch.

Turn to **264**.

342

Your Kai Discipline of Tracking reveals that the right tunnel heads east and the left tunnel heads north. You are now directly beneath Cloudmaker Mountain. Consult the map of Kalte at the front of this book before you decide which tunnel to enter.

If you decide to take the east tunnel, turn to **199**.
If you decided to take the north tunnel, turn to **284**.

343

Your enemies can only attack you one at a time due

to the narrow confines of the cell. You must fight them individually in the following order. The Ice Barbarian is immune to Mindblast.

Doomwolf 1: COMBAT SKILL 15   ENDURANCE 24
Doomwolf 2: COMBAT SKILL 14   ENDURANCE 23
Doomwolf 3: COMBAT SKILL 14   ENDURANCE 20
Ice Barbarian: COMBAT SKILL 17   ENDURANCE 29

If you win the combat, turn to **28**.

344

The fortress door is completely smooth; it has no visible lock, hinge or keyhole. However, turning your attention to the granite wall you notice that one of the massive blocks is different to all the others. A small triangle has been cut into its surface.

If you possess a Blue Stone Triangle, turn to **41**.
If you do not, turn to **147**.

345

You close your eyes and concentrate on blocking out the attacking Mindforce. You gradually control the pain, just enough to be able to tear the Bracelet from your wrist and hurl it to the floor. Cursing your misfortune, you stagger unsteadily towards the junction at the far end of this corridor.

Turn to **215**.

346

Dyce makes it across to the opposite ledge safely, although Irian slips and has to be hauled out of the glacier by his waist rope. You and Fenor are still on this side of the crevasse. It is your turn to jump.

Pick a number from the *Random Number Table*. If you have the Kai Discipline of Hunting, you may add 2 to the number you have picked.

If your total is now *0–3*, turn to **195**.
If your total is now *4–11*, turn to **232**.

347

The corridor is poorly lit and it would be easy for you, skilled as you are in the art of hunting, to approach the guards under cover of the shadows.

Covering your nose from the fumes of the bowl, you edge your way along the wall towards the unsuspecting guards. Placing the bowl in the shadow of a pilaster, you stealthily return to the kitchen to await its effect. In less than a minute, the Ice Barbarians collapse to the floor and you can approach the Hall of the Brumalmarc undetected.

To your delight you discover that one of the great jewelled doors is unlocked. Preparing yourself for attack, you gently push the door ajar and enter Vonotar's chamber.

Turn to **173**.

348

Your Kai Discipline reveals to you that there are a network of caves less than a couple of hundred yards to the south. You abandon the sledge and search southwards.

Turn to **314**.

349

During your adventure, have you discovered and kept a Glowing Crystal?

If you possess this Special Item, turn to **139**.
If you do not have it, turn to **97**.

350 – *Illustration XX (overleaf)*

As the colours fade, you become aware of a sudden drop in temperature. You now stand upon the Ljuk ice shelf at a point less than half a mile from where the *Cardonal* lies at anchor. Loi-Kymar and Vonotar are close by, both shivering in the chill morning air. Within minutes you are sighted by the ship's lookout and a longboat is despatched. As a wriggling Vonotar is hoisted unceremoniously aboard the *Cardonal* and deposited in the brig, the Captain is the first to congratulate you on your skill and daring.

'But how did you manage to return so quickly?' he asks incredulously. 'We were not expecting you for another ten days.'

'Let us say,' interrupts Loi-Kymar, 'that the wisdom of the Kai and the lore of the Magician's Guild can surpass the limitations of even time itself.'

A puzzled expression crosses the Captain's face, but it is gradually replaced by a smile as he begins to understand the magician's curious answer.

Your journey to Anskavern is swift, but you are saddened by your memories of the brave guides that were left behind. Your arrival in the port is greeted by an anxious crowd. They fear that your early return is a sign of your mission's failure. When the news of Vonotar's capture becomes known, your warrior skills are required once again; this time in the defence of your enemy against the seething mob of outraged Sommlending that assault Anskavern gaol. Safe

XX. Vonotar is led away to the deepest chamber of the Guildhall wherein lies the Daziarn: the door of an eternal prison from which there can be no escape

passage is eventually secured to Toran, where trial awaits the traitor.

Upon the dawn of the feast of Maesmarn, in the depths of the Guildhall of the Crystal Star, Vonotar the traitor is tried by his brotherhood and found guilty of his terrible crimes. He is led away in silence to the deepest chamber of the Guildhall, wherein lies the Daziarn: a portal of total darkness, the door of an eternal prison from which there can be no escape.

You are the avenger of his crimes and it is you who cast the wretched traitor into the limbo of Daziarn. Your mission is now completed. You have survived the caverns of Kalte and freed Sommerlund from the menace of Vonotar.

But the heat of battle and the challenge of a new and desperate quest awaits you in Book Four of the LONE WOLF series entitled:

The Chasm of Doom

Pacer

BOOKS FOR YOUNG ADULTS

Pick one up for a good time!

THE ADVENTURES OF A TWO-MINUTE WEREWOLF
by Gene DeWeese
(21082-2)
When Walt finds himself turning into a werewolf, one two-minute transformation turns into a lifetime of hair-raising fun!

FIRST THE GOOD NEWS by Judie Angell
(21156-X)
Determined to get a story for the school newspaper contest, ninth-grader Annabelle Goobitz and her friends concoct a scheme to win them an interview with a TV star—with hilarious results!

MEMO: TO MYSELF WHEN I HAVE A TEENAGE KID
by Carol Snyder
(21087-3)
Thirteen-year-old Karen is convinced her mother will never understand her—until she reads a diary that changes her mind!

RANDOM NUMBER TABLE

0	3	1	3	9	7	5	0	1	5
5	8	2	5	1	3	6	4	3	9
7	0	4	8	6	4	5	1	4	2
4	6	8	3	2	0	1	7	2	5
8	3	7	0	9	6	2	4	8	1
1	5	7	3	6	9	0	1	7	9
3	9	2	8	1	7	4	9	7	8
6	1	0	7	3	0	5	4	6	7
0	2	8	9	2	9	6	0	2	4
5	9	6	4	8	2	8	5	6	3